Who are you?

Ryan

I am: Blond hair, blue eyes, six foot three—all the Kids
look at me. I set the trends; I lead.
No matter what I do, I'm in; I'm graduating, getting
my full ride to college. Gonna play quarterback for
U. State. . . . Can you feel the power? I can.

Kurt

If I was cool, I wouldn't get picked on in school.
Wouldn't get kicked on, wouldn't catch shit from
everyone—seems to think it's open season on me. . . .
I can't find any more reasons to be here—hate turned
against myself becomes something really dark—this is
how it starts . . .

Tisha

*What are **you**?*
"Do you call yourself mulatto or just mixed?"
Mulatto? I'm not a mule. And *Mixed?* . . . I'm not pancake batter, either, now that's *mixed*. . . . Dumb girls.
There's nothin' wrong with me; there's something
wrong with *them*. Both sides make me strong; both
sides make me Me.

Floater

I'm so good at what I do, most people don't even
know I'm doing it. They don't know what's hit them
until they're on the ground . . . wondering how this fat
used-to-be loser not only took your money, but a piece
of your soul. They're mine, they know it, and there's
nothin' they can do about it. Now that's power.

OTHER BOOKS YOU MAY ENJOY

For: Meredith!! 3-31-04

Gr8 2 meet u!!

names

Enjoy!!

will never

hurt me

Peace & Happiness

Jaime Adoff

JAIME
ADOFF

speak
An Imprint of Penguin Group (USA) Inc.

This book is a work of fiction. Names, characters, places, and incidents are either the product of the author's imagination or are used fictitiously, and any resemblance to actual persons, living or dead, business establishments, events, or locales is entirely coincidental.

SPEAK
Published by the Penguin Group
Penguin Group (USA) Inc., 345 Hudson Street, New York, New York 10014, U.S.A.
Penguin Group (Canada), 90 Eglinton Avenue East, Suite 700, Toronto,
Ontario, Canada M4P 2Y3 (a division of Pearson Penguin Canada Inc.)
Penguin Books Ltd, 80 Strand, London WC2R 0RL, England
Penguin Ireland, 25 St Stephen's Green, Dublin 2, Ireland
(a division of Penguin Books Ltd)
Penguin Group (Australia), 250 Camberwell Road, Camberwell, Victoria 3124,
Australia (a division of Pearson Australia Group Pty Ltd)
Penguin Books India Pvt Ltd, 11 Community Centre, Panchsheel Park,
New Delhi - 110 017, India
Penguin Group (NZ), Cnr Airborne and Rosedale Roads, Albany, Auckland 1310,
New Zealand (a division of Pearson New Zealand Ltd)
Penguin Books (South Africa) (Pty) Ltd, 24 Sturdee Avenue, Rosebank,
Johannesburg 2196, South Africa

Registered Offices: Penguin Books Ltd, 80 Strand, London WC2R 0RL, England

First published in the United States of America by Dutton Children's Books,
a division of Penguin Young Readers Group, 2004
Published by Speak, an imprint of Penguin Group (USA) Inc., 2005

10 9 8 7 6 5 4

Copyright © Jaime Adoff, 2004

THE LIBRARY OF CONGRESS HAS CATALOGED THE DUTTON EDITION AS FOLLOWS:
Adoff, Jaime.
Names will never hurt me / by Jaime Adoff.—1st ed.
p. cm.
Summary: Several high school students relate their feelings about school, themselves,
and events as they unfold on the fateful one-year anniversary of the killing
of a fellow student.
ISBN 0-525-47175-8 (hc)
[1. High schools—Fiction. 2. Schools—Fiction. 3. Emotional problems—Fiction.]
I. Title.
PZ7.A2617Nam 2004 [Fic]—dc22 2003049271

Puffin ISBN 0-14-240457-8

Designed by Heather Wood

Printed in the United States of America

For Mom, who would have been so proud . . .
&
For Dad, who is

For Mary Ann & Leigh, my two favorite ladies!

&

For my wonderful editor, Alissa Heyman

"What do I have to say to the youth of America? Good luck . . ."

—*Kurt Reynolds,*
sophomore,
Rockville High

chapter 1

Walking out onto the field. I can see my breath.

The stands are packed. Faces everywhere I look.

People form a human chain around the outside of the field, from end zone to end zone.

We are home—the mighty *Bears*.

The smell of hot dogs and spilled cream soda invade my face mask.

I suck in the half-frozen air through my mouthpiece and spit.

Slow motion now. Everything the color of leaves, leaves right when they're turning, at their brightest before they fall.

Zak slaps me on the butt. We both know what's about to happen, what *should* happen.

What we've worked for, the whole season. The entire season comes down to this. This one play.

"Zak's curl on three." Even my words are in slow motion. Stumbling out of my mouth, sounding like someone else's words. Not mine. Eyes stare at me from all directions. In the huddle I am God. My congregation looking to me for salvation, looking to me for something, more . . .

I don't care if I go to hell, just throw it in the end zone.
Stew smiles. I hear his words, but his lips don't move. Did he say that or am I just trippin'?

The noise is deafening. Everyone's on their feet. I set up behind Max Steel. He's like brick and mortar. We call him House. It would take an army to move him off the line. My confidence is high. I know I can do it. Done it so many times before. Just drop back, roll to my left, and Zak will be right there, right there waiting for my pass . . . *Even slower now* . . . my feet dragging through the mud, like climbing uphill with weights tied around my ankles. Getting close to the line of scrimmage, but still, it seems like miles away. Fourth and goal at the nine. Everything is on the line. The game, the season. Everything we've worked for . . .

I have to make the play. There is no tomorrow . . .

I see the Colonel out of the corner of my eye. Standing next to Coach Johnson. He looks like a statue, frozen, expressionless. He expects me to throw a touchdown; he will accept nothing less. My father, the Colonel, accepts nothing but the best.

I feel the sweat dripping down the inside of my helmet— the pressure's on . . . It's *always* on . . .

The Norwood line is jumpy. They want me to think they're blitzing. But they wouldn't dare. Not with the game on the line. They know I'd burn them. I'm too fast, too quick. They've seen the tapes. I'm sure they've seen the tapes . . .

Back to regular speed . . .

"Ready, set, green nine-teen, green nine-teen, Hut-hut, Hut!"

Everything cool so far, dropping back . . . rolling left . . . My arm cocked back, Zak in my sights; he's all alone, waiting in the end zone, waiting for my pass. Waiting for my—

First the sound, like a freight train hitting a plastic cup. *Then,* my arm feels like it's being torn apart. The whole right side of my body is on fire. OH SHIT! I see the ball fly out of my hands and into the safety's. Zak looks like a little kid who just got his candy stolen from him. The Norwood safety whizzes past me. I see him smile as I start to fall. I'm falling. Falling fast, face first.

Falling

faster . . .

Then it's over.

Nothing but black.

Nothing.

No smells, no sounds,

Just black. The tape freeze-framed. **Me,** face first on the ground. **Number 56** from Norwood, on top of me. His body engulfing mine, like an ocean over a toy boat.

Then the tape starts again. The sounds coming alive now—I watch the Norwood safety dancing in *our* end zone. The whole Norwood bench celebrating on our home turf—I smell stale ketchup and popcorn, dirt and wet grass—everyone yelling . . .

"Get up! Get up!" Now it's a chant. The whole crowd screaming, "Get Up!!" It rattles my helmet. "Get Up!!"

"Ryan, get Up!" "Ryan, GET UP!!"

I look up expecting to see number 56; instead, it's the Colonel.

Red-faced, in his fatigues, yelling down at me.

"You're gonna be late for school. Nothin' worse than a dumb quarterback. Nobody likes them. Don't care how far you can throw, you'll never make the pros if you don't have the grades."

I try not to flinch, as each word dive-bombs from his mouth.

I guess I didn't hear the alarm.

I know he's been up for hours,
he's *always* up.

I don't think he sleeps.

Father and Son

Yeah, that's me—Kurt. Faded jeans, faded shirt, faded
face. Standing in the kitchen, starin' at my half-empty
bowl of unlucky charms. Backpack slung over right
shoulder—PANIC ATTAAK scrawled in demented black
Magic Marker right below the patch that says I'M A
LOSER, SO WHY DON'T YOU KILL ME. I'm the weird kid.
The kid who lives for metal music, hates everything,
everyone, else.

I'm probably the only one in the whole school who's
even heard of the ATTAAK. I'm an ATTAAK DOG, got
my Pound card to prove it. Gets me the best seats. Gets
me the best seats Daddy's money can buy. Money can't
buy *everything*. I mean, I know I'm strange. I feel strange
most of the time. Kids think I'm strange, too; they say
I'm a freak. Maybe I'm like what they were talkin' about
on the news the other night. Mandy Montgomery had a
special report about how people get fat. Like, they're kind
of fat, and people start calling them fat, so they eat more
and get *really* fat. Mandy called it a self-fufilling prophecy.

I mean, maybe I just started out a little weird; maybe I
was like, freak-lite—then years of being called a freak and
weirdo have made me act like a freak and weirdo. Now
I've *actually become* a full-fledged freak.

My own Self-fulfilling prophecy.

That is deep.

That is CRAZY!

I *am* a freak.

I am

Un-cool,

glasses on a big nose, sophomore-skinny body, begs for more muscle, clothes hang like they want to be somewhere else, on someone else.

I think I

s t i c k **OUT** like a sore thumb.

Like a sore . . . Mom says I'm a handsome kid. Oh yeah? Well, Mom lies.

I tell my shrink that all the time.

She says I should confront my parents. That it's all basically their fault for screwin' me up. Confront my parents? How do you confront air? They are not here. They've been snatched by beings from another planet and replaced by androids. (See, that's what I should say to my shrink; then she'd really have to work for her One hundred and twenty bucks an hour.)

My mind is wandering, but not to worry, the android playing the part of my father will soon make his *grand* entrance. Oh, here he is now . . .

"Have a good day, son." Dad's words float away on cheap aftershave and land neatly in his well-pressed suit pocket.

I just nod my head and say okay. Just let it go. Never let him know what I'm really thinking. Never let him know.

"Have a good day?" Those stupid words will stay like

a well-trained dog. They will stay in his suit pocket until
tomorrow. Tomorrow: he will reach into his well-pressed
suit pocket, pull out those ridiculously mindless words,
and say them again. The words will leave his blissfully
ignorant mouth and travel to my big-ass ears.
My ears will translate those words into:

*"I don't know who you are, I don't know what you
like, what you don't like, what you do, what's in your
head. As a matter of fact I am SO out of touch, I actually
think you're a pretty well-adjusted child. Anyway, you
live here, and they tell me you're my son, so I'm obligated
to say to you, 'Have a good day.'"*

"Have a good day?" He doesn't have a clue what I
have to go through, what I have to deal with
EVERY / DAY . . .
He should just keep his big mouth shut. He doesn't
deserve to know what I think about—how dark my
thoughts really are . . .
How close I come . . .
EVERY
SINGLE
DAY . . .

What a bond,
Father and Son . . .

Tisha's tangles

I try to comb the knots out of my mixed-up hair.
Sometimes I wish it was just Barbie-doll straight.

Sometimes I wish . . .

Mom calls up to me:

"Tisha, come down and get some breakfast. You need your energy for school."
The sound of her voice floats upstairs to my secret lair. Where sometimes I pretend I am Lisa "Lovely" Lipton, star of stage and screen. (Now, she *is* a Barbie doll.) I have her poster on my wall. Mom always frowns when she sees it. I know why. Mom thinks I want to be white, really white, like Lisa Lovely is. You know, straight hair, fair skin, blue eyes . . .
Mom's always like:

"How come you don't have Florentine Jones up on your wall or one of our great African American actresses?"
I say:

"I don't know. I don't like Florentine Jones; I like Lisa Lovely Lipton."
Mom thinks I want to *be* Lisa Lovely. I guess that wouldn't be bad; she can probably get a comb through her hair.
Not to mention all the stares from every man she passes. That wouldn't be a bad thing, wouldn't be bad at all . . .
See, Mom doesn't know. It's kinda crazy, though. At home I feel more white; at school I feel more black. Does that make any sense? I guess Mom gets scared. Thinks I'm gonna like one better than the other. Thinks I'll want to *be* one more than the other. Sometimes I feel like I'm two different flavors of ice cream, left out in the sun.

Sometimes I feel like I'll just melt away . . .

"Tisha, come down now. Your eggs are getting cold."

My name is . . .

"Mark, how come you don't bring any books to school? I mean, you're almost out the door, and I haven't seen you put one book in your backpack."

"First of all, you know I don't like that name. You know what name I want you to use."

"Look, Mark, I'm not going to call my only son, my only child, that weird name. Frankly, your father and I both think you're going a little too far with it—"

"He's not my father; he's just the guy you're currently married to."

"That wasn't very nice, Mark. You should apologize for that."

"I'm leaving now, Mom. It's been a pleasure as always. And to answer your question, I don't need them. Books are for the poor schnooks who need to study. *I* am not a schnook, and I *never* have to study. Good-bye, Mom."

"Mark, Mark, wait . . . Floater?"

The name. She said it. She finally said it. I won't answer, though. Make her sweat a little. The only thing I love more than a great entrance is an even better exit.

Oh, how I love the mornings. Can you feel it? The anticipation. It's in the air. And the smell, I love that smell. Like a brand-new car, without the car. Nature's brand-new-car smell. Hey, I like that, have to remember that one.

The smell, breathing it in deep, filling up my lungs . . . Smells like the beginning, the beginning of something big. Shit, I'm running late, have to pick up the pace. My subjects are waiting for me. There's work to be done. Lots of work to be done . . .

Ryan's morning drill . . .

"Yes, sir."
"No, sir."
"Thank you, sir."
"Good-bye, sir."

"Wait."

The Colonel moves in close. Sniffing, staring at my collar, inspecting . . . me.
I stare straight ahead, no eye contact. He's gotten worse lately. He says he misses the service; I think he misses Mom. She's been gone ten years now. Caught Cancer when I was seven, died before I was eight.
The Colonel is in my face, staring into my eyes, but I look down.
I think he's trying to see if I'm on drugs. I tell him I don't do drugs, but he doesn't believe me. The Colonel only believes what he wants to.

"You still have your *'just in case,'* son?"
"Yes, sir."

"Good. That school is going to hell in a handbasket.
You have to be prepared. Those are words to live by, son.
Always be prepared."

"Yes, sir."

"Dismissed."

Same question every morning. Always the same.
My "just in case" tucked safely away.
Safely, away . . .

I walk out of the house, as normal as I can. Too fast and
he'll think I'm scared; too slow, he'll think I'm lazy. I
look over my shoulder, and the Colonel is sitting in his
favorite chair, reading the paper. I open the front door; he
doesn't look up.
He's done with me,
for now . . .

Kurt *never* misses the BUS

While all the stabbing cuts and hate rake me over the
coals.
While all the stares and cackling laughter burn a hole
through my soul . . .
My mind goes to her.

I feel the sting before I hear the smack. The back of my
neck gets hot, like someone lit a match on it and now
my skin is burning off. I feel the outline of the handprint
starting to form.

"Hey, Dirt, I mean, Kurt, watcha gonna do? You gonna do somethin' about it?"

"Freak boy looks like he's gonna cry."

"You gonna cry?"

"Let's see some tears, you fuckin' freak loser . . ."

The taunts and shouts blast into my ear, I take out my CDMan and crank up PANIC ATTAAK. I'm in the midst of a Misty Manic meltdown, her sultry voice from hell riding me over the bumps in the back of this bus. But Misty is not the face I see. I see *her* face.

"Hey, Dirt, why don't you just die? You know you want to, I bet you've tried . . ."

Not loud enough.

I turn up Misty a little more and reach into my coat pocket. I pull out *her* picture.

The one she gave me. Actually, the one I took.

We were sitting in biology class. Tisha was getting out her book when the picture fell on the floor. I grabbed it. See, I always sit close. Sometimes she looks my way. But I always turn my head. I know she's not *really* looking at me. Probably just trying to see what time it is. Probably trying to see anything

but

me.

Maybe someday I'll say something to her. Maybe someday I'll say, "Hey, how are you?" Something she'd expect me to say. Something normal. I'm good at pretending to be normal.

I'm good at pretending.

Like now, I'm pretending I can't hear them. I'm pretend-

ing all I can hear is the ATTAAK. I'm pretending everything is fine.

Everything is

not

OK.

One tear escapes, trying to make a break for it. Running
for the fence, streaking down my cheek . . .

Its salty taste makes me thirsty.

I shut my eyes and swallow hard.

   Why don't I say something back? *Open up your*
mouth. Make them cry.

Say what I really feel . . .

SAY SOMETHING—

SAY SOMETHING.

But I don't.

Never do.

   I just sit on this bus and take it. I just sit and take it.

But

Her smile and Misty Manic's scream make my torture a
little bit better, a little bit easier to swallow—all this shit.

Just

a little bit . . .

chapter 2

Nose—Eastern Europe
Lips—West Africa
Hair—somewhere in between
Order more:
self-esteem

"Hey, Tisha, watcha' doin'?

"Hey, Tiny. Just chillin' till first period."

"You look like you starin' hard in that mirror."

"Naw, just checkin' my makeup." *My makeup. Shoot,
I wish Clarke's sold noses at the lipstick counter.*

"You cool. How 'bout me?"

"Yeah, you cool, too, Tiny."

"You know what today is, T?" I pretend I don't hear
her. I don't want to hear her. I've got enough to deal with.
I try to stall as long as possible but Tiny keeps on.

"Earth to Tisha, did you hear me? You don't wanna
hear, that's it, huh? Well, it's not gonna change nothin' by
trying to ignore it."

"Yeah, I know what day it is." I finally answer, my
voice sounding foreign, like it's coming from someone
else.

"You still think about it?"

"I try not to." *Maybe if I don't say much, she'll stop
talking about it.*

"One year, today, I can't believe it. Can you believe it's
been a year already? He would've been a senior this year.
Wonder if they're gonna have somethin' today? Maybe a

service or somethin'." Tiny is talking into the sink. She keeps on talking as she rubs her hands underneath the faucet. Keeping her focus on her hands and the running water. Her words not as important as what she's doing.

I don't feel like talking. All I can do is stare at the water dripping out of the faucet.
Dripping out,
drop,
by drop.

This faucet is always leaking. I don't know why they don't fix it. All I want is to get the image of Jake's dead body out of my head. I shouldn't have looked in that bathroom. They were just putting up that yellow tape. His body twisted, his face frozen with pain. We were just laughing together the day before. He told me a funny joke in study hall. I can't even remember what it was now.
That was the first time I really talked to him. I don't care what he got mixed up in. He didn't deserve it.
No one deserves *that.*
I am trying to force that day out of my brain, let it pour out, into the sink, down the drain. *I can't believe it, a whole year already . . .*

"Hey, Tisha, we gotta get on outta here. *You know who* and her friend will be here any second. T, come on; we gotta go . . ."

Before the bell
Can you feel the power?

I can.
Everything changes as I turn from boy
to
MAN
walking through the double doors,
down the main corridor . . .
A rush of adrenaline courses through me. It's game time.
I see the field, everyone coming towards me, trying to get
a piece of me. They want to get close, hoping some magic
might rub off.
I smile to myself as I walk towards the lockers.
I am walking and thinking . . . Playoffs on my mind,
The Norwood game and my sweet Susie Sunshine . . .
Can you feel the power?
I can.
Senior magic, that special quality only stars have. I am the
best; I am a star.

"Hey, Ryan, what's up? You guys are gonna kill 'em
tonight."

"What up, Ry?"

"Hi, Ryan . . ."

And on and on. I don't need to answer. I just nod. It's
understood. It's respect. Something you get when
you've put in your four years, and now you're looking at
college ball—everything I wanted, everything *we've*
worked for.
All these years . . .
I am:

Blond hair, blue eyes, six foot three —
all the Kids look to me. I set the trends; I lead.

"Born leader," the Colonel says. He's right; I am. I love
this feeling. It's right here in my hands—right here in my
mouth. I can taste it.
I go to class but I don't have to. No matter what I do, I'm
in; I'm graduating, getting my full ride to college. Gonna
play quarterback for U. State. I worked hard for four
years; now I deserve a little fun. I deserve to do what I
want to do. I'm a senior and seniors rule!
Can you feel the power?

I can.

Before the bell
Principal Roberts's
Morning Announcements

"Good morning, students.
As most of you are already aware,
today is the one-year anniversary of the death of Jake
Stiles.
For those of you who are freshmen, Jake was a beloved
student here at Rockville High.
There will be a short memorial service in the cafeteria
during sixth-period lunch.
Also, there will be voluntary reflection and meditation
before third period.
Our school counselor, Mr. Tanner, will be available for
walk-ins, so please don't hesitate to knock on his door.

There will be a reporter from 7 Alive News here today.
You may speak with her between classes, during your
study periods and lunch. However, you are not obligated
to speak with her, so don't feel any pressure to do so.
Remember, students, we always want to portray
Rockville in a positive light. This is a great school. Let's
be proud of it!"

   "One last item.
I want to see everyone at the game tonight, eight p.m.
kickoff. It's playoff time, folks, our first step towards our
third Championship in a row.
For all you freshmen, this is your chance to see the
mighty Bears in postseason play. I have been told by very
reliable sources that we are going to *destroy* our arch
rivals, the Norwood Tigers, tonight. Let's all come out
and watch the mighty Bears put the cats to bed.
There will be a tailgate rally for all students, teachers, and
parents starting at five-thirty p.m. in the south parking
lot.
Let's show some school spirit!!

   "Goooooooooooooo
BEARS!!!"

   "Thank you, and have a wonderful day!!"

Before the bell
Back to the bathroom, starring Tisha & Tiny & Cheryl & Vicky

You know who and her friend, otherwise known as
Cheryl and Vicky.

Oh, they'll be here, and soon, too. If Mom only knew
about Cheryl and Vicky. She thinks it's all good now,
since we moved to the suburbs. She thinks everything's
cool now, especially with the girls. She thinks they won't
slam me like they did in the city. Just because Mom and
Dad are upwardly mobile doesn't mean I'm going anywhere. My situation hasn't changed a bit. Not one bit.
I'm still gettin' ready to be stuck in this bathroom, gettin'
ready to get slammed. Mom thinks these kids are more
educated, more sophisticated. Shoot, they're more
screwed up, that's what they are.

See, I should have left the bathroom right away. Any
other day, I would've been thinkin' clearer.
One-year anniversary . . . The words keep replaying
in my mind. The image of Jake's lifeless body in the
third-floor bathroom—playing like a movie clip I can't
stop.

See, I should have left outta here right away, that's what
I should've done. Tiny tried to warn me. She always
knows when somethin' bad's gonna happen. I should've
listened to her.
Now it's too late . . .

See, maybe Jake had it easy. At least he got it over with. I get killed a little bit every day.

Right now, right here in *this* bathroom. Oh yeah, it's about to happen; it always does.

Here it comes . . .

"What we got going on in here?"

"Looks like Zebra Girl and Big Momma."

I wanna say:

"Hey, stupid, my name is Tisha Reznick. You want some of me?" But I don't, I never do.

"Damn, I know you two aren't tryin' to look pretty, 'cause that's just not gonna happen. You better step away from that mirror. You might get fourteen years' bad luck between the two of you . . ." Vicky moves towards us, getting in between me and Tiny.

"I think maybe they sweet on each other. You two sweet on each other, huh? You can tell us, we won't tell anyone."

"That's nasty, Cheryl. Those two make me wanna puke . . . especially that fat one . . . damn, how you get that fat?"

"And what about this mixed-up one? Tryin' to act all black and stuff. We should just give you a real 'sister' beat down. Then we see how black you are. See if that white girl don't come runnin' out, cryin', beggin' for mercy. How would you like that, half 'n' half?" Cheryl's sour breath is starting to make me gag. Her face is so close to mine, I can tell exactly what she had for breakfast. *Rotten eggs* . . . I try to turn away, but I can't. I feel like I'm going to be sick.

The laughter is like bars in a jail cell. Keeping me prisoner. Paralyzed. I could've made a break for it when they first came in, but now it's too late. They got me trapped. I look into Cheryl's eyes, just for a second. All I see is hate, nothin' but hate. Why do they hate me so much?
I'm brown just like they are.
Vicky's got Tiny boxed into a corner. I feel so bad for her. Tiny looks scared. Sweat is pourin' down her face, tears streaming down her cheeks.
Vicky's got her shirt pulled up over her stomach, smackin' it, laughing at how big it is. I want to just yell at Tiny, tell her not to cry. Tell her it'll be worse on her if she cries. But I can't. No words come out of my mouth.

Then it ends, as quickly as it began. The first bell rings and they run out of the bathroom.
Vicky gets one more smack in, and Cheryl pushes me down as she runs out the door.
I look up at Tiny, and she looks at me. I try to speak, but I can't.
No words come out of my mouth.
No words . . .

We don't look at each other as we walk out of the bathroom. Soon we'll pretend it didn't happen—like we always do. That's how we get through. We'll start talkin' like everything's cool, Tiny will make me laugh, and that'll be that.
But we both know it's not over yet . . .

we both know . . .

Maybe
today.
Maybe I've just been on a bad losing streak.
Maybe I'll get to my locker and there won't be **FREAK**
written all over it. Maybe I've hit rock bottom. Like the
stock market did—nowhere to go but up.
See, *that's* a good sign. I'm halfway to my locker and no
one's said anything bad to me yet.
Actually, that's strange, everyone seems to be preoccupied
with something else.

"What's going on?" My question floats above the lockers and lands on top of Matt Dumont, a Senior. He looks
at me like I'm a roach and all he wants to do is step on
me. He just stares, like I'm from another planet, the
words I'm speaking from some language he's never heard.
A wicked smile Etch A Sketches its way across his face.
He looks at my busted shoelace and slams his locker shut.
Never saying a word.
So I got dissed by a Senior, that's nothing new. Nothing
compared to the bus. Nothing compared to all the other
stuff I have to deal with. I can handle that. If that's the
worst I'm gonna get.
Maybe today *will* be different—OUCH! Hot sting to the
back of my neck. Followed by two more. The four-finger
smacks hitting their mark.
Can't see who did it. Tons of kids everywhere. Donald
Newton is laughing right in my face. He didn't do it, but
I can tell he knows who did. I know there's a big red
mark on the back of my neck. I don't rub it. I pretend it

doesn't hurt. I open up my history book and look for something to distract me.

On the first page in big red letters somebody wrote, KURTS A UGLY FREEK FUCKIN LOSER. Well I wanted to be distracted . . .

I take one last look inside my locker—I touch my gym bag. I want to take it out but I don't, not now.

I walk slow to first period.

No matter how hard I try—no matter how hard . . .

Fuck it.

Maybe today will go fast . . .

Maybe.

But I know it won't . . .

Fly on the wall

Vice-Principal Paul Shavers: Is all this security really necessary?

Principal Ronald Roberts: We are not going to have a repeat of last year. I know they talk about lightning striking twice, but I don't care. Anniversaries have significance, percentages rise—we all caught a break last year. All things being equal, we should all be out on the street right now. If it wasn't for the Stiles family—

VPPS: Listen, Ron, I don't think we should get too carried away here. How much is all this going to cost anyway? I mean, the metal detectors alone set us back a bunch. We've already got twice the number of security guards as we had last year. I just don't see the need for more. I really think today is just another day.

PRR: Relax, Paul, the money for the extra security isn't coming out of the school budget—we've got some very generous alumni.
Besides, the security is just my backup. I've got eyes and ears in this school, remember? I know the kids we need to watch . . . I'm confident we'll head off anything, long before it happens . . .

chapter 3

I am first, period.

I know every answer to every question on every test, on every homework. You can't give me a pop quiz. I see it comin' a mile away. I've handed in my homework, my quiz, and next week's project before most kids have taken their coats off. I'm a genius, the one they call Floater. That's because I move in and out on my own ocean. Waves I've created. I'm like the moon; I've got my own gravitational force, and there's not shit anyone can do about it.

MiSSion sTateMent: "I'm beyond you." That's my most famous line. I'm known in twelve different school districts for that line. I get e-mail from kids I don't even know for that line.

"I'm beyond you." I love what that does to a person. It's like a snowstorm, an instant snowstorm. Paralyzing you, your wheels stuck in two feet of instant thick powder, fallin' straight from my Cerebellum—landing on your unsuspecting, just-out-of-the-shower, first-period, wet freshman hair. I give you one of my patented "Floater stares." Frozen. See, now the kid is frozen. All I have to do is touch that kid and he disintegrates. It's like watchin' a kid walk into a cold lake. Watchin' the water fill up his shoes, first soaking his socks, then his feet. The water getting so deep, the kid's almost drownin'. But I save him. I throw him a bone. A life preserver.

"I'm beyond you, but I'll help you." See that's the life

preserver. I help the kid out of a jam. Usually he needs an answer, sometimes a whole test worth of answers, sometimes a paper. Sometimes, something else. I'm the one who can get things. I'm the one who can get things done. I'm the one.

I float between all the cliques, all the groups. See, I can slum it with the dumb kids, feed their souls with some hopeful trash-talk about how easy the next test is gonna be, and for a fee, well, let's just say they may pass to see another day. I float upstream to the smart kids. Make the nerds feel cool, like they actually belong. Make them believe they may actually be able to get laid before the end of the year. Oh yeah, they love to hear that. See, I keep the peace. Well, really they police themselves. See, I do something for a kid, he does something for me. It's not *all* about the money.

At any given time I may have an army of spies, working off their debts. There's always someone at the right place at the right time. Well, almost always . . .

This place isn't a school; it's more like a prison. More like a zoo. See, I float between races, too. Keep it all from blowin' up. Have to keep them separated, but together. Black, brown, white—everyone's got an angle, everyone's got a price. Everyone needs somethin'. I *am* Johnny-on-the-spot. The kid with the golden tongue. I've worked my way up through the ranks, earned my place in the hierarchy of High School life. Roberts thinks he saved me; it was *me* who saved *him*. He needed me, things were getting too out of hand. He needed another set of eyes, another pair of ears. I was the perfect choice. Who would ever think me and Roberts were a team? Kids assumed I wasn't even smart. That's because I kept my mouth shut and watched. Watched the futility of their *class* system.

Roberts doesn't like to show it, but he knows. Deep down he knows . . . I am the best thing that's ever happened to that man. You better believe I deserve to be where I am. I've eaten my share of shit over the years. Now I don't dish it; I give a kid a choice. See, that's the key. A kid's always got a choice. Free will. Free, well, sometimes, sometimes it's gonna cost you. I solve problems, like math equations. There's always an answer, always a solution. See, I provide a service.

What's in it for me, you say? Besides cash? One word. Access. I get access. I walk into Principal Roberts's office, no appointment necessary. I'm in on everything. I get to give my two cents' worth. Matter of fact, *they ask* for my two cents. I'm allowed to run my business, as long as I give some crumbs to the powers that be. You know—I wash *your* back; you wash *mine*. Just don't drop the soap—hey, that was a good one. I'll have to remember that.

Anyway, I was talkin' about the powers. See, knowledge *is* power. The powers, they love that. They like to know what's goin' on, you know, at street level. Like, who's doin what to who, and what are kids talkin' about. What's about to go down; how can it be stopped. Stuff like that. I guess in this day and age, they want someone on the inside. Someone who can warn them *before* the shit hits the fan. You may ask, what happened last year. Well, that was a breakdown in communication. I tried to warn Roberts that something was about to go down, but he didn't want to hear. Sometimes the truth doesn't set you free, it holds you hostage . . . Anyway, those thugs were caught. They weren't even students here. Roberts learned his lesson that time. He won't make the same mistake twice.

A quick note to my detractors: Some kids like to say that I'm a legend in my own mind. That I'm all talk . . . I don't really have all this power. You know what I say to that?

Nothing. Not one word. The more they talk, the deeper they bury themselves. One call from me and they've got a week's worth of detentions. If they're dumb enough to question my authority, then they can just rot. See if I care. **Enough about that—back to ME:**

Some might say I'm a snitch. That I'm tryin' to play both sides. I prefer to call myself an ambassador. A political consultant, with diplomatic status. Sometimes I'm asked by the powers that be to intervene on their behalf. Sometimes it may just require a word or two, sometimes something more, something stronger. Situations may dictate for me to subcontract my work out. It is rare, but there have been occasions when brute force has been necessary to resolve a problem. I don't like violence; it makes me break out. I hate to break out. So violence is a last resort. I tell myself it's for the good of the school. The good of the school? Who am I kidding? I could give a shit about the school, and the school could give a shit about me. As long as they get what they want, they leave me alone, so I can get what I want. I'm sixteen years old and I'm makin' more money than all the kids here, *combined*. Cash, tax-free, and clear. I've got more influence than the mayor, more perks than a bouncer at a strip club. You'd think I had it all. Well I do, almost. I still have to report to Roberts. He tries to keep me down, likes to put me in my place from time to time. I'm just looking for my chance, my one big break. My way out from under Roberts.

But for now, I keep quiet and do my job. Quite well, I might add.

Mrs. Fields is calling the roll, but I'm not done yet, I haven't gotten to the big finish. This class is too easy, I should be in American history 3 but I decided this better suited my needs. Gives me a chance to catch up on the more *pressing* matters at hand.

(Okay, here comes the big finish.)

The big finish: I'm so good at what I do, most people don't even know I'm doing it. They don't know what's hit them until they're on the ground, starin' up at the clouds, wondering how this fat kid with the fat face, this kid, so out of shape, who in any other setting would be on the receiving end of daily butt kickings—how this (Okay, let's tell it like it is) fat used-to-be loser not only took your money, but a piece of your soul. I love that look, the one they give me when they know that I've squeezed them. They made a deal, and now I've come to collect. I've squeezed them so tight that every breath they take from now on is gonna be like an asthmatic tryin' to breathe in a smokestack. That look of utter disbelief, a kind of terrified wonder. They're mine, they know it, and there's nothin' they can do about it. Now that's power.

"How is this all possible?" you ask. "This can't be true," you say, as you try to walk slowly away, backward, taking small cautious steps. Not trying to look directly in the eyes of this brand-new twenty-first-century spy . . .

My answer?

Simple. I'm a genius and

I'm beyond you.

Remember?

1st period
Ryan's patch of sunshine . . .

On my mind, my sweet Susie Sunshine. She's across the hall, different class, but this first period is the best, 'cause I know she's thinking about me right now. While I'm *stuck* in American history 2. Her blue-and-gray backpack is resting on the floor, her cool yellow jacket lying on the back of her chair. Her short brown hair bouncing up and down as she laughs her Susie Sunshine laugh.

This first period is the best, 'cause I know after the bell rings we will meet by the water fountain and I'll sneak a kiss on her cheek and she will sneak a hug, squeezing my varsity letters close to her chest. And then we will hold hands, walking down the hall to second-period science. Everyone will look at us. They'll smile and say, what's up? I'll just look cool, don't need to do a thing. Senior privilege. Captain of: our ship. I'm the best. That's the way it is, the way it will always be.

On my mind, Susie Sunshine, as Mrs. Fields calls the roll:

"Ryan Duncan."

"Here." I say in my laid-back Varsity Voice. Third-row cool—me and Zak and Stew. We are the elite. We're going to Three-peat.
The BEARS. We *are* the Champions!

"Kurt Reynolds." He's one of *them*. I don't even notice him. Why should I? I don't look back. They shouldn't be in class.
Don't know their names. Don't care. They're not really there.
They
don't
even
count.

This is my school. My class. My town. Don't want "them" around. They just bring us all down. Make *us* look bad. That's what the Colonel says, but it's true. They make *us* look, at *them*, on purpose.
Now I'm all mad. They're killin' my Susie Sunshine buzz.

Her face is love. Her face is love. Her face is on my—
Oooh, so goood. Sometimes in the girls' locker room— my secret place. Sometimes in the boys'.
Sometimes . . . who am I kidding, all the time. Whenever we can. Grab a handful of love, grab a handful of heaven, grab a handful. Knee deep in Susie Sunshine, my patch of sunshine . . .

> *If I was cool, I wouldn't get picked on in school.*
> *Wouldn't get kicked on, wouldn't catch shit from*
> *everyone—seems to think it's open season on me.*
> *Laughter behind my back follows me home on the*
> *bus. They're not laughing with me—at me. Attacking*
> *with smirks, and words hurt, you know. Sticks and*
> *stones break your bones, but words can kill your*
> *soul—explodes with every put-down, every beat*
> *down. Shards of broken self-esteem cutting up all my*
> *dreams—welts on my mind from fighting my self*
> *against my self. I become less than everything, every-*
> *one else. I used to be me, now just a fraction of a*
> *piece of a part of the whole. I can't find any more*
> *reasons to be here—reasons not to fear—hate turned*
> *against myself becomes something really dark—this is*
> *how it starts—and it's only*
>
> *first period . . .*

I like that poem. Just wrote it. I think I'll put it in my
greatest *hits* notebook.

Otherwise known as my hit list. Yeah, there's lots of cool
stuff in that notebook. Poems and songs and . . . names of
kids and teachers who I wish would just . . . disappear.

"You've got so much potential, Kurty, you're just
throwing it all away."

Mom's words.

"You've got so much potential, Kurt, you're just throwing it all away."

Mrs. Fields's words.

"I don't give a shit."

My words.

"Kurt Reynolds."

"Here."

Almost the only word I say all day.

Nobody even looks. Nobody even cares. They're either trying to kick my ass or freeze me out.

Can't have it both ways, have to pick one or the other.

I mean, it's all bullshit anyway.

Separation:

of

the

masses: *You* go there, and *you* go there. Each kid has to fit into a box, has to fit into what's taught. Teaching us to walk in between the lines—in between the lies.

Jocks, drama queens, prom kings,

and me.

You know what? Why should I care? I shouldn't, but I do.

I am trying to maintain some sense of

I am trying to make some sense of

my life.

Every day the same old shit.

Every day

on

the

Inside:
I'm a swirling tornado of hate and misplaced *good*—used
to be there, but now, just bare trees. Dead leaves,
eaten by bugs.
but
on
the
Outside:
I'm calm. To the untrained eye I seem alright. Just
another kid. Sitting in the last row of first-period history.
I look normal, on the outside/ I would almost *be* normal
if I didn't feel like shit all the time.

Phil Stevens asks if I did the homework. I tell him no.
I could've, though. It was easy. I guess you could say Phil
is my only friend. He's pretty cool. As cool as *we* can get.

I don't care. I hate school, it's just a waste of time. I do
what I have to—to get by. Just enough to keep my folks
off my back. They don't care anyway. Never ask to see my
grades. I just tell them I get B's. That's enough for them.
Sometimes Mom likes to put on a show, like she cares. It
doesn't last. It's all just a show, just a show . . . Phil wants
to know if I want to go to his house after school. Says he's
got some cool new video games. I tell him I just want to
go to California and watch the waves. Phil makes a face.

I just want to watch the waves. Like I did when I was
small. Nothin' to watch here except the corn growing.
I'm always surprised that no one's actually died of boredom. I mean really *died of boredom.*
I guess there's worse ways to die.
I'm drifting off . . . thoughts bouncing in and out/crash-
ing against my brain, like waves.

Mrs. Fields is looking at me like I'm a stranger. Like she's never seen me before.

Maybe she hasn't.

Maybe, I'm not even here.

Are the Kids Really Alright?

Mandy Montgomery: Okay, Bobby, are you ready?

Bobby the Cameraman: Okay, I'm ready. In three, two, one . . .

Mandy Montgomery: This is Mandy Montgomery, 7 Alive News, reporting from Rockville High, where today marks the one-year anniversary of the shooting death of Jake Stiles.

It's first period here at Rockville High, students are getting ready for another day of learning, but is that all they're getting ready for?

Looking out onto this sprawling suburban High School campus, one question comes to mind. Could this happen again? Could another murder like that of Jake Stiles happen again, here, at Rockville High?

Today I am going to try and get an answer to that question, and I'm going to get that answer from those who would know best. The students themselves.

As I walk past these seemingly endless rows of lockers, each locker representing one of our youth, I say to myself, what happened? What went wrong? Are we really out of touch with our children?

So now, please come and join me on my mission, as I try to find out, one year later, **Are the Kids really alright?**

BTCM: Okay, we got it. Remember they want to go live for the first interview, and at lunch.

MM: I know. I told them it wasn't a good idea, but does the newsroom ever listen to me? No, of course not. Morons . . .

8:10 A.M.—
the question asked again:

What are you?

A person.
  No, I mean what are you?
A human being.
  Why do you look like that?
Like what?
  You know the way you look?
How do I look?
  You know, different.
Different?
  Yeah, your hair, doesn't match your skin, doesn't match your name.
Is this some kinda game? What am I, a pair of socks?
  You gotta pick a side. Them or us?
Who is them and who is us?
  If you're not with us, then you're with them.
Understand?

*What are **you**?*

Now I have to deal with this junk? It just doesn't stop. *These* girls, Tammy and that other one, at least *they're* all talk. They won't push me down, like Cheryl does, or twist my arm like Vicky. These girls, I don't know, they *might* be worse.

"*Tisha Reznick.*" Mrs. Fields calls my name.

"Tisha Reject," they say, laughing and snickering. They just love to start stuff, asking me dumb questions like:

"Do you call yourself mulatto or just mixed?" *Mulatto?* I'm not a mule. And *Mixed?* . . . I'm not pancake batter, either, now that's *mixed*. Dag, wish I would have thought of that comeback in time . . .

Dumb girls. Don't know nothin'. Mom says they're just ignorant—their parents are ignorant, too. I don't know what's true anymore. Especially in this school. They make it seem like something's wrong with me. There's nothin' wrong with me; there's something wrong with *them*.

I'm proud of me. I know where I come from. Granpapa Saul worked till the day he died, just so my dad could have a better life. Granpa Henry moved up from the South, put down roots, and had one of the first black-owned stores in his neighborhood.

Both sides make me strong; both sides make me Me. They say, I'm not really black, not really white, either. I say, I'm both. I'm *bi-racial*. But they don't wanna hear that. They say I talk black, but I look white. They say I dress black, too. How do you dress black? Shoot, I tell 'em, I talk how I talk—hip-hop, my dress matches my walk. Cool, like that MC Mini P—you know, the ninth-grade sensation from MTV.

"Fuck your family tree," Tammy told me. Don't think I haven't tried to make them understand. These girls don't wanna know, don't wanna know a damn thing.

"They're just jealous," Mom always says, trying to make me feel better.
Jealous of what? Shoot, I can't bring myself to tell Mom what *I* see when I look in the mirror.
How I see this girl so out of place. In between *everything* . . . Short and tall, round and small.
Nothin' growin' up top, either. Hips spreadin' out, too. (That's nice!)
They call me the white Afro—*No, I'm not.*
I am kinky blond hair and a mocha-brown face.
They say I'm a white girl with a tan that never fades . . .

Granny calls me a super combo. I don't know, I feel more like an unhappy meal. I just don't fit in; I just don't fit. Not in this school. It's mostly white, but all the black kids stick together. Both sides want me to choose, but both sides don't *really* want me.

All these chicks are whacked-out anyway. I mean, I don't look at *your* skin before I can be your friend. But this place, everyone has to be in a box—be like a pair of socks. Matchin' with everyone else. You know, the smart with the smart, jocks with the jocks, geeks with the geeks, freaks with the freaks. But what about me?
Where do I fit in?

"You gotta pick a side": There goes Tammy again. Tryin' to get me mad. Wants to get a rise out of me. I just want to be left alone. Let me be. Let me sit in this chair.

Leave me alone. I try to ignore her but I can't. She leans in and whispers it again.

"You gotta pick a side": I can't, doesn't feel right. To say I'm all white or all black. I'm both. But they don't understand. You'd think they would. Everyone talkin' about multicultural, and whatever. Sounds good on the news, but in this school those are just words, got no meaning here.

It's crazy though, really—like Daphne Smart, sittin' over there, third in, second row.
I know for a fact she's just like me. But she says she's black, so she fits in. Well, she looks more black, too, but what's that got to do with it? She picked a side, so she gets to slide.
I don't care, that's wrong. I mean, if she says she's black, doesn't that just erase one half?
Like one whole part of her doesn't exist. All those struggles, and sacrifice, erased. Like going in my history book and tearin' out all the pages that make up half of who I am. Tearin' pages out of history, just to fit in. I don't know, I don't think that's right. I don't care what they say, I'm never gonna do that, but these kids, they make it so hard. Hard to be what I am. My life *would* be easier if I did pick a side. Sometimes I wonder what that would be like . . . Sometimes I—
wonder what he's lookin' at, always starin' at me. That boy, Mark somethin'. He calls himself Floater. I caught him checkin' me out. Tiny thinks he likes me. Whatever. I mean, I may not get many dates, but he is *definitely not* my type. Besides, he's kinda creepy, too.

Last week he said he could make all my problems dis-

appear. I was like, "*What* are you talkin' about." He just
smiled and gave me his card. He said he could get me in
with all the cool girls. He said he could make me the most
popular girl in school. He actin' all cool, like he was *all
that* and stuff. I mean, what's a boy in high school got a
card for, anyway? He's such a geek, too? What's he tryin'
to do, hit on me?

Then there's that one, Kurt—he thinks I didn't see him
scoop up that picture of me. I saw him reach down on the
floor, tryin' to be slick. Pickin' it up and puttin' it in his
pocket like it was somethin' *he* dropped. I pretended I
didn't see. I wanted him to have it. When I first got to
this school, first day, walkin' up the stairs I tripped and
dropped all my books. Everyone passed me by. He was
the only one who stopped to help. Picked them all up.
Didn't say a word, just looked down, like he didn't want
me to see his face.
Anyway, we never even spoke. Don't know if I should
say somethin' to him, maybe just hi,
I don't know, we'll see.

Dag, first period goes *so* slow . . .

chapter 4

She's a pretty one. That one there—Tisha, such a nice mix, very sexy, too. Oh, the things I could do for that girl. She's having a bit of an assimilation problem, I think. Having a bit of a hard time. I extended an olive branch . . . but— she'll come around. Oh, she'll need something that only I can get her, then that will be my chance. I don't like to feel sorry for myself. I know my limitations. I know what I can and cannot do. A girl like *that*, I would never stand a chance, on an even playing field. But who says I play fair? It's not how you play the game but whether you win or lose; that's what I always say. Sure it would be nice if she liked me, for me. But, that's not reality.

I can accept that. I've accepted worse. Bottom line, she *will* be mine, just like everything else I've gotten in this school. I'll get her, too. Maybe not today, but one day, I will.

I will . . .

Just hang in there . . .

"Kurt, are you with us? Kurt? Kurt? . . ."

"Okay, you got a break this time, class, read up to page one twenty-two in your American history chronology books. Be prepared for Monday. You never know what you might find when you get to class . . ."

The bell saved my ass, again . . .

Maybe on Monday everything will be reversed.

The opposite of the way it always is.

Yeah, on Monday I'll walk into school, I'll be cool and popular, and everyone who slams me—will be gone . . .

Or

Maybe

Maybe Monday morning the bus will crash and only me and Phil will survive. And all the kids that laugh and put me down, they'll be gone,

gone forever.

Mr. Tanner's words come in loud and clear, into my head, I know just what he'd say:

   "Now, that's pretty dark . . ."

He'd say it with a smile and turn his head towards me, like he really cares.

I think he does.

Mr. Tanner's voice drifts through the noise of screeching chairs and slamming books. The bell ringing loud, but not loud enough to drown him out.

Me and Mr. Tanner having our talk, in my head, as I get ready to leave class.

   "Okay, Mr. T, how about I save Tisha from the burning bus, but I leave the other kids screaming in pain . . ."

   "Kurt, you're a smart kid. You can't let them get you down. You have to stay up. You have to try to stay positive . . ."

Everyone likes Mr. Tanner. I think he's pretty cool. Much cooler than my shrink. He doesn't even make half as much as her. A high school counselor can't make much, can he? He says, "It's not about money." That life isn't about money. Tell that to my parents. He said, "Okay." But they never called him back . . .

Mr. T says, if I just hang in there, things will turn around.
Just hang in there.
I'm trying to.
I'm trying to stay positive, even though,
even though—
I don't know,
it's just so
hard.

Quarterback sneak

My eyes follow Becky Boswell from her chair to the
door. Actually, it's her butt that catches my eye.
A thing of beauty—a heart-shaped ass. Got that from this
old flick I saw once. This dude has this affair with this hot
girl; they do all kinds of kinky stuff. Anyway, he tells her
she has a perfect heart-shaped ass. Becky's got one, too.

This is my fatal flaw. My one weakness. I don't share
this with the Colonel. He would say what he always says.

"Women are the downfall of mankind. Keep your pants
zipped and you'll go far . . ."

I'm in love with Susie; this is for sure. But I just can't
help it. Like with Kim. I couldn't help myself. I thought
she wanted me. She did but . . .
I think she's mad. Won't look me in the eye.
Still, I would try again . . .
Becky is *so* fine. Look at her, she knows it, too.
And yesterday was *amazing. I've got to see her again—*
I know Susie is right outside the door. I have to be quick
about it, if I'm gonna do it. In one motion, I get up and

stride towards her. My words warming up on the side-lines, ready for the play. I say,

"Hi, Becky, I was kind of zoning out when Mrs. Fields told us what chapters to read. Can you help me out?" As I speak, I drop the note into Becky's half-opened back-pack. She sees it all happen, watching me run my play flawlessly. She answers me, but I don't listen. I nod and act like I'm writing down what she says. She scribbles something on half a piece of paper and rips it out of her notebook. She drops it on the floor. I drop my pencil and pick them both up. I glance quickly at her note—*Let's do it again.*

She read my mind.

I walk past her without saying a word.

Damn, I'm good . . .

Tisha Sly-ding down the hall . . .

> *You can make it if you try . . .*
> *You can make it if you tryyyyyy . . . .*

I turn the volume louder on my CD Man; now Sly is the sound track to kids changing class. It's like my own mini-movie. Makes the walk to second period more fun.

> *All together now,*
> *Yeah, yeah, yeah,*
> *Yeah, yeah, yeah . . .*

I love Sly and the Family Stone. Been listening to them

since I can remember. Mom and Dad always had them playin' in the house. They were so cool. Their music, what they were saying. And the band, it was like the first integrated rock band. They brought all these different types of music and people together to create something brand-new and exciting.

Like me, *brand-new and exciting*.

I am smiling and singing as I walk down the hall. I'm lucky, most of my classes are in the north wing. It's only a hop, skip, and a Slyyyyd to Mr. Baker's English 2 class. I'm acing it anyway, so I can take my time.

Tammy is shaking her head at me as I walk by. I feel the other stares, too. Most kids don't know what to make of me. They just don't know me. That's the problem—they don't *try* to know me. I'm still smiling but I'm getting that feeling in my stomach again. The one that tells me, I'm not *really* new and exciting, I'm just plain old Tisha, who doesn't really know who she is or—

"Hey, T, lemme guess, Sly?" Tiny says, a little out of breath.

She looks like she was *workin'* to catch up to me.

"Oh yeah."

"You crazy, girl, listenin' to that old stuff." Tiny rolls her eyes. She doesn't like to admit it, but she likes Sly, too. I caught her listening to him a couple times.

"I like the new stuff, too, it's just Sly always gets me in a good mood," I answer back. I feel better now that Tiny is with me. I don't know how she does it; she always shows up right when I'm starting to feel down.

Tiny is leaning in towards me as she talks. I know she's trying to hear Sly. I give Tiny her cue and she can't resist, we both start singing at the same time—dancin' down the hall to second period.

You can make it if you try,
You can make it if you tryyyyyyy . . .

Floater makes an offer they can't refuse.

"Terrence, Marvin, Stanley, where's the other one?"

"Who, Leonard?"

"The kid with the stutter who got busted for hacking into the NSA mainframe two years ago."

"Yeah, that's Leonard."

"Where is he?"

"He's home, sick."

"Okay, whatever. We only have a few minutes before second period. Who's got my money?"

"Ah."

"UH . . ."

"Mmmmm . . ."

"What is this, everyone forget how to speak? Let me ask you again. Who's got my money?"

"That would be Leonard."

"Look, I don't have time for games. You go send an e-mail or a text message or sync up your freakin' Palm pilots to a satellite, I don't care. You just tell that geek of nature, Leonard, if Floater doesn't get his cash before the end of the day, everything is off. *Capisce?* No protection from the jocks, no more of those *videos* you like so much—nothing. You guys have been maintaining a very nice quality of life here at Rockville, thanks to *me*.

But that can change.

If I don't get my money, you guys will be running for cover, diving back underneath those keyboards you crawled out of, and sleeping in your hard drives again.

Do we understand each other? Good.

Now get outta here.

You three are creeping me out, you look like ghosts.

Don't you ever go outside?

Get some sun, for Christ's sake . . ."

Hallway politics . . .

Big kid:

"I need you to write my paper for me. It's due tomorrow."

small kid:

"I, uh, I . . . I, uh, I don't know, I could get in trouble."

Big kid:

"Let me put it to you this way: if you don't write my paper for me, I will

kick your ass."

small kid:

"I'll have it for you in the morning."

Me and Susie

walking hand in hand, I can feel her rays on my face.

I pull her body closer to mine. My sweet Susie Sunshine
is *so* cool.

She doesn't have to say a word, it's all in her smile—takes
away all the bad, everything that's sad. Susie is the best,
everybody knows that.

She is the best girlfriend a guy could *ever* have. Sexy and
strong—by my side. They should teach her body in Art
class. The way she walks and her soft sexy talk makes me
craaaazy.

Nothing is wrong when she shines . . .

Her rays, keep *him* OUT. But not for long . . . The
Colonel is too strong . . . too strong . . .

The tape starts where it always does.

*I hear the crack of the belt before I feel the pain. The
sound telling me to just sit and take it. Don't yell; it will
only make it worse. The buckle digs into my back, raising
the skin on impact. I sit there, feet dangling over the edge
of the bed. Enduring this ritual, again and again.*

The Colonel mumbling unintelligibly.

*He gets up, acting like nothing happened, goes into the
kitchen, and starts dinner.*

Susie squeezes my hand tighter, but not tight enough to
bring me back,

not just yet.

The Colonel, always telling me who I'm supposed to
be,

what

I'm supposed to

do.

I do what he tells me,

what he tells me to do.

Me and Susie pass a few of *them*.

"Losers," I say under my breath.

"Have to rise above the scum, and the lowlifes of the world. Have to rise above it all. Stomp out the fires of weakness, so they do not burn down our house of God. Have to rise above." The Colonel—serious words from a serious man. He hates weakness, hates that I have to go to school with all these loser kids. They have no future. He says, they are nothing.

Nothing.

Second generation: Strong. Made this country what it is. Have to keep this country what it was. Proud. Duncans are proud. We don't run. We don't hide. We don't lose. We always win.

"Can you say that, son? Duncans always win. Duncans always win."

The Colonel's words reverberate, rattling every bone in my body. Making the hair on my arms stand at attention. His words on the refrigerator in the kitchen, next to the shopping list and the word of God.

"Duncans always win." I say it with military precision. Discipline.

My dad, the Colonel. Takes no prisoners. Shows no weakness . . .

"You okay, babe?" Susie asks, seeing I've gone away for a minute.

"Yeah, I'm fine." I return, face to the sun, her rays shining bright, makes me feel like we're the only two people on earth. Sometimes, I wish we were . . .

chapter 5

Mandy Montgomery: Now just relax. Just answer any way you like.

Typical teenage student: Okay.

Mandy: This is Mandy Montgomery, live, here at Rockville High School with just a taste of my new hard-hitting report **Are the Kids really alright?** I'm here with a typical teenage student, a sophomore at Rockville High. She has asked that we do not give her name.

Let me first start with this: Do you think things have changed in the year since Jake Stiles was murdered?

TTS: Not really. People kinda chilled for a minute, but basically, everyone's still doin' the same stuff. You know, doin' what they wanna do.

MM: And what are some of the things kids *wanna* do?

TTS: I don't know if I should say, don't want to get into trouble, you know my mom might see this.

MM: This is the news; you can't get into trouble for this.

TTS: Yeah? You don't know my mom . . .

MM: Thank you for your time. This is Mandy Montgomery reporting live from Rockville High.

Bobby the Cameraman: Okay. We're clear.

MM: That went really well. Geezus, we're going to get a negative rating if all the interviews are that bad. I knew I should have stayed in bed today . . .

2nd period PANIC ATTAAK

"Kurt, did you hear? *They're* coming . . ." David Sorin's highly medicated whisper infiltrates my ear canal. Well, at least *he* takes his meds. I shouldn't be so hard on him. He tries, like me, both of us on the outside; but David, well, he's *way* outside. Always wants to start a conversation with me.

"Yeah, I heard. I already have floor seats," I whisper back. Trying to sound less annoyed than I really am.

"Cool." David's left wrist is twitching as he picks up his pencil. See, that's what it does to you. Turns you into a hyper twitched-out loser.

I'm already a loser, so why do I need the side effects? Mom would freak if she knew I stopped taking my meds. That's the one thing she cares about. She says I'm just so much better since I've been on that baby Prozac. I just act like it's helped me. I know what it's supposed to do, so that's how I act around her. I even have my shrink fooled, but that's not hard to do.

I've got everyone fooled. That's the one thing I'm good at.

I'm like a spy . . .

Nobody knows who I really am.

Not even me . . .

I try to ignore David, closing my eyes. Watching Misty Manic in my mind, riding her Harley onstage. Revving up the engine, screaming at the top of her lungs. "ARE YOU READY TO BE ATTAAK'D?"

"Hell Yeah!" the crowd screams. Misty rev's her motorcycle engine again.

"Hell Yeah!" I hear the drums beat in my head. The first chords explode from Vini Viper's guitar. I am in the "pit." Away from this school, from this class—from my life . . .

I can't wait for the ATTAAK.

I can't wait.

Random sampling
Fear

"Alright, class, today we are going to talk about fear. Why we have it, where it comes from, and what are our biggest fears. What are our fears, on this day, the anniversary of one of our own, being murdered? Are any of you guys scared? Scared you might get killed, just scared of your own mortality? Anyone? Kevin?"

"My biggest fear is that I'm going to get hit by a car because I'm not paying attention, because I'm starin' at some girl's butt . . ."

"*Thank you, Kevin. Thank you, we really appreciate that.*"

2nd period
No regrets . . .

English lit is so boring. Who reads books anymore? I wonder what Roberts wants. Vice Principal Shavers said it was important. Probably has another list for me. Another one of his Psycho lists. The kids with question marks. The ones who might explode. Roberts is all freaked out by this one-year anniversary thing. I told him not to sweat it . . . Isolated incident, I told him.

He didn't want to hear that. I'll calm him down. I've got it under control.

Principal Roberts, man, if people only knew, underneath that tough facade beats the heart of a pussy . . .

He'd be lost without me.

Lost, without *Floater* . . .

I guess I should be a little thankful. He did pluck me out of *relative* obscurity, giving me the opportunity to re-invent myself. Maybe just a *little* thankful.

"Mark, I'm going to change your life." Those seven words, the sweetest words I'd heard up to that day. Roberts had his eye on me for some time. He said he saw the trouble I was having. He says trouble . . . I say I was getting the shit kicked out of me every day. Anyway, I sat down in his office that fateful fall Freshman morning, listening to my future flow gently from his lips, the words dancing across his desk on their way to my ears.

They say salvation can come in many forms. Mine came in the form of a jaded, paunchy, middle-aged, slightly paranoid high school principal who was constantly worried about getting fired. I listened as Roberts laid out his plan to me. Telling me how he needed a smart kid like me to let him know what was happening in the school. What was *really* happening. Yes, he recognized my intellectual prowess, but he also knew I was the most desperate kid in the freshman class. I was an easy mark. (Pardon the pun.)

Roberts went on . . . Saying that if I helped him out, I would never get beat up again. I would never get picked on again. As a matter of fact, he said, "Kids will want to be *your* friends."

"*My friends*," I said back to him in my innocent freshman falsetto. It sounded too good to be true. Some of it was. But Roberts was my only chance. I took it and never looked back.

I've got no regrets,
no regrets at all . . .

Ryan needs some sunscreen · · ·

Behind the last row of lockers there's a wall, then a small space.
Then there is *my secret place*.
Construction STOPPED in the girls' locker room . . .
ran out of money halfway through . . .
I know how to get in. Just have to crawl a little. But it's worth it.

Oh yeah, it's worth it.
I call it my love room.
It's a little dusty but it will do. Haven't had any com-
plaints yet.
Well, maybe Kim, but that's ancient history. That's the
past.
I'm not worried. She'll be back. They always come
back . . .

Right now: I can't wait
between second and third, my midmorning break.
Paged my sweet Susie Sunshine.
Our secret code . . .
S

      E

           X

Soon I will have her easy-access dress in my hands.
One-touch control. Global command.
Bra strap will snap—fast. Pants will unzip—quick.
Then it will be *on*.
Slow and easy . . .
does it . . .
easy . . .
does . . .
I sit in my secret place and
wait for my sweet Susie Sunshine.
Her body burns
so good . . .

My midmorning break. Eight minutes of freedom.
Eight minutes of hell. I know what's coming. That's the
worst part.
I know that I can't hold it anymore. I have to piss. I
should have gone before first period; now it's almost
third. If you're like me, you try to avoid bathrooms like
the plague. A Rockville bathroom is *not* the place to be.
It's kinda funny watchin' all the kids do their dances,
walking all bent over by the end of the day. All bent over
from holding it in.
Kind of funny until it's you. Well, now it's *me*. I miscal-
culated, drank too much grape juice before school started.
Lost myself in the ATTAAK. Now I have to piss real
bad. Nothin' I can do about it. When you gotta go, you
gotta go.
I look both ways before I walk into the bathroom, like
I'm crossing the street. Making sure no one follows me in.
I think I'm safe. I should've known better.

"How much you got, loser?"

"Hey, Dirt, what's that on your pants?" Matt Dumont
is smiling his sinister smile. The one that says, I know
something you don't know.
His eyes are like black ice, hard and dark.
That's the last thought I have . . .
before he pushes me
over
   the
      back
of another kid.

I fall flat
on
the
floor.
trying to
c
atch
my breath,
Catch my
breath,
catch my
Death.
My wind knocked out of *me*—kissing the nasty bathroom
tiles.
After the pain is gone: the real hurt comes. They take my
money,
take my pride—piss it away . . .
flush it
down
the
drain.

Pathetic . . .
I'm lying frozen on the gross bathroom floor, as Dumont
picks over me like a vulture working on a carcass.
Hate consumes me now—starts to tear away at my well-
crafted coping mechanisms. My real feelings boiling up to
the top, but I won't let them break through. I keep them
down, keep them stuffed, locked away.
Like my gym bag, locked in my locker . . .
I smile and get up slow,

wiping the grime off my pants with a wet paper towel.
Other kids come in and out. Some stare; most look right
through me.
I'm the invisible man.

Can *you* see me?

chapter 6

This is Mandy Montgomery, continuing my exclusive report **Are the Kids really alright?**

Mandy: I am here at Rockville High with junior Myra Livingstone.

Vampire: It's Myrna.

Mandy: Oh, sorry, Myrna Livingstone. Myrna, some may say that the way in which you dress could be interpreted as threatening. With your so-called goth clothes and spooky makeup. Are you trying to make some kind of statement?

Vampire: This is just me. You know, it's who I am. If I'm trying to make any kind of statement, it's that I am an individual who has the right to dress any way I want to.

Mandy: That may be true, but how much of an individual are you when there are twenty to thirty other so-called goths walking around campus as well?

Vampire: I must have started a trend.

Mandy: Try not to turn around during the interview, thanks. We're going to edit all of this later, but the less work the better, okay? Let's continue.

So you really don't find the manner in which you dress threatening in any way? I mean, if I were a student I would sure as heck steer clear of you ... I mean, if I saw you walking down the—are those fangs you have in your mouth?

Vampire: MMMMMMMMandy, I bet you taste sweet. Let me have a look at your neck ...

Mandy: Okay, Bobby, cut. This girl is creeping me out. Can I get a kid here who's halfway normal? Geeezus ...

The coolest girl in the world

is wearing her white lab coat like it's a Kat Carlisle designer raincoat. I don't know how she does it. She just makes everything look good. She's so cool. I wish I was like her. Even her name is cool—Monica Drake. Now that is a cool name. Only Monica could look cool helping Mr. Thomasan set up for third-period lab. She breezes past me in the hallway like she's a queen on her way to a royal dinner. She always dresses so sharp. Lots of kids have money, but most girls here still don't know how to dress right. Monica Drake always looks good. She is always put together just right. She looks like those models in the glamour mags. The ones with those perfectly fitting jeans and tops that always match. I wonder how many tops she has in her closet. I never see her wearing the same one twice.

Monica's got that star power, she just walks past you and you turn your head. Girl, boy, doesn't matter, everybody looks; even teachers look. They try to act like they don't, but they do. She's just got it. I watch Monica pass by and I feel so dumpy compared to her. Wearin' my wannabe hip-hop clothes. I never know what matches. Mom always has to help; she says I'm a little color-blind.

I try to stay close to the classrooms during break . . . Cut my chances of getting slammed. Monica's hand touches my shoulder as she passes by. I think she wants me to move. Maybe some of her coolness will rub off on me. Infect me with a cool bug, a cool virus with no cure.

"Hey, Tisha, download this." Tiny starts talking in my ear. Like anyone can hear us during midmorning break. I start laughing; Tiny always cracks me up. Talkin' all her stuff about boys. You wouldn't think to look at her, but Tiny gets all kinds of boys. Seems some boys like big girls.

Huh, go figure. I couldn't get a date in this school if you paid a boy to go out with me.

Monica drops a beaker on the floor. Me and Tiny smile at each other.

She's even cool when she messes up.

We've got our backs to the wall, facing the lab room. We keep one eye on Monica and one eye on traffic. Never know when Cheryl and Vicky might try to creep up and slam us. This way we can see what's goin' on.

Monica glides by us again. She smells good, too. I want to smell like that. Reminds me of spring. Like lilacs or something. Wish it was spring now.

She doesn't even look at us, as she floats past. She always acts like she has somewhere important to be.

I don't know, maybe she does.

I luv

how she tastes—wet kisses on my tongue.
I luv how she smells and feels and I can't ever get enough.
I feel like I'm all sex and sweat and football forever.
Walking down the halls, nothing can stop me.
Not *him* or them or
any team anywhere in the world. I luv how she tastes,
how she smells,
how she *feels*.
Susie is all that. She is everything. She is it.
We are the perfect team . . .
I got it all planned out.
Already signed my letter of intent.
Goin' to U. State. Susie is, too.
I'm gonna go pro, then we'll have it all.
We will have the best
of everything.

In the Office

Principal Roberts: Hey, Mark, why don't you have a seat.

Floater: Mr. Roberts, how's it going?

Roberts: Oh, not too bad, how about yourself?

Floater: Pretty good.

Roberts: Good. Well let's get to it. You're aware of the significance of this day. I want it to go as smooth as silk. It is *not* an option for something to happen today. We've got a news crew here. If there is even the smallest of incidents, a lunchroom fight, anything, you know that reporter will be all over it.

Floater: No doubt.

Roberts: Here. These are the names of students we've had our eyes on. We don't have anything on them, but we feel they represent a threat.

Floater: So what do you want me to do?

Roberts: Do what you always do, Mark. You have a *way* with these kids. They listen to you. I just want you to keep your eyes open, watch, listen, find out what they're up to. If need be, have a little chat with them. If anything seems out of the ordinary, you come and tell me directly. I know you've seen all the extra security around campus, I don't want you to talk to them. I am going to stay in control. That's how I've lasted this long at this school. That's how I'm going to continue to last. I know I can count on you, Mark. You've never let me down in the past.

Floater: I won't let you down, sir. I'm on top of it.

Did you see that?

Did you see what just happened there? In Roberts's office. How smooth I was. Did you see how it was *me* who was in control, not him?

"So what do you want me to do?" I asked him.

I know exactly what he wants me to do. I just like hearing him say it. I get off on that. That power. I have the power to make or break anyone in this school—do you realize that? I could tell Roberts so-and-so is planning to do something, or this person is acting weird or strange. One word from me and that's it. The kid's life is ruined. ForEVER. Now, that is serious.

Roberts, he doesn't have the stomach for it. I tell you what, if I give him someone on *this* day, I won't have anything to worry about . . . ever. I can write my own ticket, all the way to graduation. I won't have to report to him anymore, won't have to report to anyone. I will have total autonomy.

It will be my world, my universe, and everyone else will just be living in it . . .

Just a game

I am trying to make myself small, standing outside third-period lab. Tiny is all in somebody's business at the water fountain. She loves to eavesdrop. She'll fill me in later, I'm sure. Corey Taylor from my geometry class is staring at me as he talks with his friends. He looks kinda like Donovan, my ex, from my last school.

Hair is different, but they kind of favor. Donovan, he was so vain. Must have looked at himself ten times a day in the mirror. I should have been hurt when he broke up with me, but I wasn't. I don't think he *really* liked me.

I think he just wanted to say he had gone out with a black girl. I kept trying to tell him he was going out with a half-black girl, but he never got it. I would say I was bi-racial, and he would look at me like I was speaking a different language. I guess that should have bothered me more at the time, but I let it go. I really liked all the attention, and it felt good to actually have someone like me. *Me.*

"Hey, Tisha, what's up?" Corey Taylor looks me up and down. I can't tell if he's making fun or being real.

"Hi," I say back in my little voice—the one I use when I don't know what to say, which is most of the time.

"You going to the game tonight?" Corey is staring at my chest. I don't know why; there's nothing there.

"I dunno, maybe." My voice getting a little bigger.

The bell rings and Corey is still staring at my chest, his lips are moving, but I don't think he even cares what he's saying.

"Cool, later," he says, and walks toward his buddies. I see Corey lean in and say something to his friends. They look at me and laugh. See, I knew he was just playin' me. Boys do that all the time. I think they try to see if I'll take the bait—they just want someone easy; I don't even think it's about looks . . . it's all just a game.

Just a big fat game . . .

In the middle of a quick visit with Mr. Tanner

"Are these kids actually doing physical harm to you?"

Is that a trick question? How am I supposed to answer that? If I tell him the truth, then I'm a snitch and things will be ten times worse. If I lie, like I always do, things will never get better.

"No, of course not. It's, I don't know, it's just how they act towards me."
There, back to the safety of the lie. I had no choice. I can tell he doesn't believe me.

"Kurt, what happened to your pants?"

"I don't know, I guess I fell. They were ripping anyway."
He is totally not believing me. Come on, say something, stop staring at my pants.

"Alright, we'll talk about this some more next time. We've gone into third period. I'll write you a note for your class. Look, Kurt, I'm glad you stopped by, and if you ever want to tell me something, get something off your chest, you know my door is always open."

"Thanks. I know."

"I'm sorry we only had a few minutes, but since we missed our last appointment, I just wanted to make sure you were okay. Are you okay, Kurt?"

"Yeah,
I'm okay . . ."

3rd period entry
Floater's file:
Sandwiches and confessions

I listen. Sometimes you can listen without hearing anything. I watch and listen to the unheard words. Body language. How a kid shifts in his seat can tell me more than
what comes out of his mouth. I watch reactions. I love it.
I watch.
You know, the building crescendo of kids talking before
class, about this or that, loves lost, won,
sex, drugs . . . Sometimes they spill their guts, sometimes
it's just their lunch. Sandwiches and confessions fall out of
backpacks, crashing to the floor, waiting to be swept up
and thrown away. I just found out Kate's not a virgin
anymore. That's a news flash. Rab and Joey got high
before school started; Joey's folks are out of town. And
so on, and so on . . .
Some kids are spooked about it being the one-year
anniversary. Most, though, don't seem to even notice. I've
got my eye on one of the kids on Roberts's list. He's way
on the edge. Word is, he's got some kind of hit list. Kids
say he gets beat up a lot and never fights back. I don't like
to hear that. Those are the scary kids. Those are the *real*
scary kids . . . Scary, but . . . he could be the one. The one
I've been waiting for. He could be my ticket to freedom.
My all-access pass to absolute power . . .

I'll just watch him for a while. See if he exhibits any telltale signs. You know the never see it comin' behavior. That's the thing with these kids; you really don't ever see it comin'. It's never the ones who act out in class. No, it's the quiet ones, the kid who just sits there and takes it, day after day, month after month, year after year, until one day, he pops. *This* kid could very well pop; then again, he may not. Doesn't matter, I can make it seem like he will. Oh yeah, I feel my genius kicking in again ...

Roberts is so paranoid, he'll believe anything today.

He's still so obsessed with the whole Stiles hit. I tried to tell him that was a pro deal. Jake got caught up with some seriously unsavory characters.

It was a very unfortunate incident, for everyone ... but it won't happen again.

We squashed that drug pipeline, at least for now. Roberts is still scared, though.

Maybe I'll just let him stay that way.

Keep him afraid while I work my

Floater magic ...

Kurt's wish

Sometimes I wish I was like what you see in the movies. Hand in hand with the pretty girl. You know—gettin' the girl in the end. I like when they zoom in real close on their faces. The way they look at each other. Their eyes all glazed over. I wonder how you get that glaze. I only get that glaze when I get mad. But that's different.

I always sit next to Tisha, but I might as well be in

another room. I drop my pencil on the floor and pick it up, slowly scooting my chair closer to her in the process. I don't know why I torture myself.

I can almost taste the words on my tongue, the words I want to say, the words that choke me on the way up, on the way out they get stuck in my throat. They always get stuck . . .

When I see *her*, something happens on the inside. I feel weird. Like I'm scared and excited at the same time. My heart starts beating fast and I feel like I can't breathe. My stomach starts doing somersaults. Sweat breaks out on my forehead. Sweat breaks out everywhere.

On the inside, something happens. Something good, I think . . .

Sometimes I wonder if I'll ever get a girl.

I guess girls think I'm weird or whatever.

I mean, I've had a girl *like* me before, a long time ago, but I blew it as usual. I didn't follow through. I didn't even try.

Tisha has her head down, she's writing something in her notebook. That spot on her neck. It's sooooo sexy. The nape of the neck is supposed to be one of the most sexy parts of a woman's body. I heard that in a movie once. I don't know about with most girls, but in Tisha's case it's true. I wonder what she would do if I kissed that spot, right now. Probably slap my nose off my face . . . It would be worth it . . .

She reminds me of Misty Manic from PANIC ATTAAK. They have the same kind of hair, but Tisha is much prettier. I wonder if Tisha can sing?

Why can't I say something? I am sooooo lame.

This is my chance—right now, it's just me and her. Her friend Tiny went to the bathroom. All I have to do is just say hi, anything.

But I can't, you know why? 'Cause I suck. That's why . . .

I hope I get paired off with Tisha for the lab. Then I'll be forced to talk to her.

Come on, Mr. Thomasan, say, *Reznick and Reynolds, Reznick and Reynolds . . .*

Hurry up, before Tiny gets back . . .

"Reynolds, Manning, pair off." Mr. Thomasan's booming voice shatters my plan. Manning? That kiss ass from the front row? Now I'm gonna have to move up *there*. I won't even be *close* to Tisha.

I feel myself slipping again.

Mr. Tanner says to imagine a big ladder, and when I feel like I'm slipping, to reach for the ladder and try to pull myself up.

I'm reaching,

I'm reaching.

Biology Bar be que

"You two have fun while I was gone?"

"Tiny, you're always tryin' to start somethin'."

"Hey, I see how you look at that boy, what's his name, Kurt?"

"I don't look at him. How do I look at him?"

"I don't know, I'm just sayin' I seen you look at him like maybe you like him."

"Tiny, you're trippin'. Watch what you're doin'; you're liable to burn the lab down."

"I tell you what, I wish I had some burgers. I'd put them right over this Bunsen burner. We could have a bar be que."

"Tiny, you are so crazy . . . I swear . . ."

chapter 7

Mandy Montgomery: Hi, this is Mandy Montgomery here at Rockville High School, where I am continuing my exclusive report **Are the Kids really alright?**
I am with a senior here at Rockville who wishes not to be identified, so we are going to block out his face. What should we call you?

Student: You can call me Mr. Cool.

Mandy Montgomery: Okay, uh, *Mr. Cool*, do you think things have changed at Rockville in the year since Jake Stiles was murdered? More to the point, do you think it could happen again?

MC : Look, Mandy. Can I call you Mandy? Cool. Well, in my opinion, nothing has changed since last year. I mean, you can still get drugs, guns, anything you want. It's as easy as pulling up to the drive-through at Hamburger Halo.

MM: Are you saying you can get drugs and guns right here at the school?

MC: Well, maybe not right here, but there are people at this school who know people who can get you *anything*. I wasn't surprised at all when Jake got capped. If you piss off the wrong people, bad things can happen.

I hate to break it to you, but there's some heavy drug stuff going on in this community. You got your party drugs, pot, X, coke is still around. Then you got crank. I can tell you where a half a dozen meth labs are, just within ten miles of where we're standing right now.

It's supply and demand and, like the kids around here, the demand is *high*.

It's crazy, I'm tellin' you. People say crack is back. Shit, crack never left. Oh, my bad. You can't say *shit* on TV, can you?

MM: It's okay. We can edit that out.

MC: Look, I got to go. I'm supposed to be in study hall. I have to get back before the bell rings. I just came out to get something from my locker. You were, like, lurking in the shadows. Trying to catch people off guard, huh?

MM: Okay, Bobby. I think we've got enough here. Thank you, uh, Mr. Cool. I appreciate your time.

MC: My pleasure. Hey, Mandy, I have to tell you, you are like, even more smokin' in person . . . you want to hang out later, after school?

MM: I don't *think* so . . . BOBBY!

Rockville High Times
Bully's corner
no. 1

> ### HE
>
> *looks different*
> *acts weird...*
> *must be a loser*
> *must be a geek*
> *must be a freak*
> *what should we do?*
>
> "KICK HIS ASS!"

Rockville High Times
Bully's corner
no. 2

> ### SHE
>
> *looks different*
> *acts weird...*
> *must be a loser*
> *must be a geek*
> *must be a freak*
> *what should we do?*
>
> "KICK *HER* ASS, TOO!"

I watch Zak and Stew *tear up* Fu Manchu.
He's trying to leave, but they won't let him.
Don't know what his real name is, doesn't matter.
I join in on the fun. Just laughing in his face, squinty eyes looking up at me,
trying to find a way out.
Sorry, dude, can't help you.
He has to go to the bathroom. Raised his hand, got his pass—
but that's not what he needs now.
Guess he won't be getting an A today.
Stew whispers in my ear.

   "Hey, Ryan, let's see if he goes in his pants."
Fu Manchu looks horrified, about to cry. Zak laughs.
I join in. Hold his hands down.
It's a fine art, keeping him prisoner without Mr. Rose seeing.
I know it's wrong, but I go along.
The Colonel says, "They're all just gonna' take our jobs anyway.
The Orientals are making it hard for *us*."
Why shouldn't I make it hard for *them*?
Finally, Mr. Rose asks Fu Manchu if he's going to use his pass.
Fu Manchu looks at us.
We laugh and let him go.
Fu Manchu gets up fast—trying to cover the dark wet spot on his pants.

"Damn, that was fucked up," Robbie Toll says. Robbie, Mr. Politically Correct.

"So what?" Stew stares hard at Robbie, shredding the kid with his eyes.

"So what . . . ?"

"The Situation"

Vice-Principal Paul Shavers: What are you going to do about the "situation"?

Principal Ronald Roberts: I don't think I have much of a choice.

VPPS: Have you called anyone in yet?

PRR: Not yet. I've been sitting here trying to figure out a way around this thing, but I can't.

VPPS: What about the kid?

PRR: I haven't decided yet. I guess it should come from me.

VPPS: I can't believe it.

PRR: This is all I need, today of all days. I never catch a break, do I?

Hi, Tisha

How are you?
Hi, Tisha, what's up?
Hi, Tisha, did you do the homework?

Come on, I've got to say something to her. Third period's almost over. I have to say something now.
Okay, 1, 2, 3—

"Alright, folks, please return all equipment to the front and have a good weekend. Don't forget our lab practical on Monday. Maybe you could at least pretend that you know what you're doing this time . . ."

That's it. Mr. Thomasan messed me up. Damn, she moves fast. I was just about to say something to her . . . Who am I kidding? I wasn't going to say shit. I am such a loser.
I suck.

"Get out of the way, Dirt." I feel the push before I hear the words.
I can't breathe.
Suffocating.
Mouth is dry like the desert.
I need a drink.
I have to get out of here
NOW . . .

The water fountain

Water splashes on my face as I lean over to take a drink.
I feel a little better now. Always feel better outside of

class. In the hallway, there's more space. More room to breathe.

I suck down the water, slurping every drop. Hey, there's Tisha . . . I lift my head up. Maybe I'll catch her eye. I should have noticed the two kids plotting off to the side. Now it's too late. Somebody yells:

"DIRT"

and there goes my face. My face. Slow motion, over and over again. That familiar metallic taste. There goes my face. My face into the bottom of the water fountain. My face in with all the spit and the phlegm, my face in with the boogers and dead skin.

My face in the bottom—

with all this nasty shit, all this nasty spit, I swallow—can't help it,

I swallow, and gag, and choke,

here comes the undertow . . .

Slow

motion

rewind

over and over

again . . .

There goes my face

my face

in the bottom

my face

in the bottom of the water fountain.

An hour goes by in my mind, but really only a few seconds. I lift my head, and see everyone staring at me,

pointing at me, laughing at me.
I feel like I'm gonna puke.
I'm pretty sure I'm gonna puke.
I'm gonna
puke.

chapter 8

Mandy Montgomery: Okay, Bobby, did you fix it? Good. I'm sorry about the delay. All this technology and nothing ever works . . . What did you say your name was?

Rachel Brooks: My name is Rachel, Rachel Brooks.

MM: Okay, Bobby, I'm ready. This is Mandy Montgomery back at Rockville High, with more of my exclusive report **Are the Kids really alright?** I am here with Rachel Brooks. Rachel, why don't you tell me a little about what life is like here at Rockville.

RB: I dunno, it's okay, I guess. I mean, it's a huge school. Teachers are okay. Students are okay, most of them, at least. I mean, I didn't even know this Jake kid. I wouldn't even associate with someone like that. I'm just trying to get into Plymouth. That's where my father went, and his father before him.

MM: Tell me, Rachel. Do you feel that conditions are right, here at the school, for more violence? Or do you think things have changed?

RB: I dunno. Like I said, I've got my own stuff to deal with. I mean violence, that can happen anywhere, can't it? I turn on the news and there's violence everywhere. Why should it be any different here?

MM: Good point, but in light of the shooting last year, do you think something like that could happen again?

RB: Ms. Montgomery, pardon my French, but the world scares the shit out of me. These days, anything can happen, anywhere, anytime. All I know is that I want to graduate, get out of this place, and get into Plymouth. That's all I know.

MM: Thank you, Rachel. Thank you very much.

Tisha's trip to 4th period . . .

I hate goin' to fourth period. My biggest trek of the day, have to go all the way from the north wing to the south. Don't have Tiny to hang with, either. Have to be by myself. Have to look over my shoulder all the time, too. Make sure no one's tryin' to creep up on me. All these kids, and I feel alone all the time. Nobody talks to me; nobody tries to help you here. Everyone on my heels, goin' up the steps. One false move, and I could trip and fall . . . One false move . . .

He is sooooo fine. That Ryan Duncan boy—what a bod. *Now that is one fine white boy.* I can hear Tiny; that's exactly what she'd say. I start to smile and then—

"You better keep your eyes in check, if you know what's good for you."

Beth Cochran's voice comes out of thin air and hits my ears without warning.

"That's Susie's man. Don't get any ideas. I know, where *you're* from, that kind of stuff goes on, but not here."
I try to say something, tell her I wasn't doing anything wrong, but before I can, Beth goes *there*.

"You people are always trying to take our men. Well, we're tired of it. That stuff doesn't go here. You understand?" *You people?* Back in the city that girl might get capped for talkin' like that. Beth pushes past me, nose in the air like she doesn't even want to breathe the same air as me. Her straight blond hair brushes my face. I see her shake her butt as she climbs up the stairs. Shakin' so every guy will see, acting so superior to everyone, so superior to me.

I should push her. I could, too. She's right in front of me. All I have to do is give her a little shove and get lost in the crowd. Nothin' to it. Easy. I don't think I'd *really* do it, but it makes me feel good thinkin' about it. Makes me feel real good.

Other girls look at me as we climb up the stairs. They stare, at me. Stare at my face, at my hair. I know what they're thinking. They don't have to say it. I can see it in their eyes. I can see it. Shoot, if I told Dad about this, he'd be pissed. I can hear him yelling.

"All those years of struggle, lives lost for the cause, and this is what we have to show for it? Our only child having to be subjected to these narrow-minded, ignorant, racist kids." That's his speech, heard it lots of times. I won't tell him, won't tell Mom, either. It'll just make things worse. Found that out back home. Found that out a lot. We moved from a small town to the city, and now

we're in the suburbs. I don't fit in anywhere. I think
Mom and Dad thought things would get better for me
each time we moved, but they didn't. They just got
worse. I don't want to disappoint them anymore. Just
gonna keep all this to myself. Just gonna have to deal. At
least I got Tiny. We're in it together. Me and Tiny against
the world.

Listening in

"Ryan, do you love me?"

"Of course I do, babe. You know that."

"No, I mean really love *me*, Suzanne Jacobs."

"What are you talking about, Susie? I love everything
about you."

"I know, but sometimes, it's just—"

"Just what?"

"I don't know. Sometimes you seem so distant, is all.
Like you're not all here. I don't know, maybe I'm just
imagining things. I know you're under a lot of pressure
with the game and everything and—"

"Nothing I can't handle. Let's talk about this later;
you're going to be late for class. Here, give me your backpack."

"My all-American, taking control. I like that . . ."

"That turns me on when you say that."

"I know it does."

"Maybe it was someone else, Beth."

"No, it was him and Becky Boswell. Yesterday—mid-morning break. He didn't think anyone was in the locker room. I was in the stall. They disappeared around the last row of lockers."

"He was in the girls' locker room?"

"Yep."

"He is *such* an asshole. Does Sooze know?"

"Not yet."

"I don't know why she's still with him. This isn't the first time, you know."

"I know."

"When are you gonna tell her?"

"Not sure, probably at lunch."

"Let me know, I don't wanna miss it. She's gonna FREAK!"

"Yeah she is . . ."

Floater: . . . Hey, I'm just sayin' sometimes grades can get changed. Computers make mistakes, especially if someone enters the wrong grade. Come on now, Phil, play ball. This is coming straight from the top.

Phil Stevens: Look, I don't know anything about Kurt having a hit list.

Floater: Phil, Phil, Phil. Why are you protecting this kid? I know you're friends with him but maybe you guys are *more* than friends. Maybe it's something *more*, Phil. Is it, Phil? You two got something going on together?

Phil Stevens: Get outta here with that stuff.

Floater: You do, don't you? Wow. I'd hate to have that rumor hanging over my head. Spreadin' through school like a virus . . . Talk about killing your sex life. I mean, you're not exactly a ladies' man, but with that rumor going around, you'll never get laid . . .

Phil Stevens: Come on, man. You know I don't go that way. You wouldn't do that to me. Would you? Hey, hey, wait up, okay, I . . .
I might have heard something . . .

"Frank and I did the best we could. We loved Jake
more than words can say. He just got mixed up with the
wrong crowd. I can't believe it's been a whole year.
It seems like it was just yesterday . . .
I still can't believe my baby's gone . . ."

Pre-taped Voice of Mandy Montgomery: That was
Denise Stiles, mother of slain Rockville High student,
Jake Stiles. You can see more of this exclusive interview
with Denise Stiles as part of my special report **Are the
Kids really alright?**
Tonight on 7 Alive Nightwatch . . .

Russ in the studio: Thank you, Mandy. Now let's go to
Cloud Davis with the weather. What's it doing out there,
Cloud? . . .

chapter 9

Now it's fifth period.

Some kids are eating lunch, I'm eating puke.

Puke went up my nose, so I'll probably smell it all day.

That's me, Dirt. I am puke.

"Get yourself together/Keep yourself together,"

Misty Manic screams into my ears, as I try to get the taste of vomit out of my mouth.

I take out a warm Coke from my backpack and take a quick drink.

Seat down, sitting on the toilet, feet up, so no one can tell I'm here. I've been stuck in this position for a whole period now. I just can't seem to move.

The smell of grease and sickly sweet pie is mixing with my vomit—here it comes again . . . SHIIIIIIIIT!!!! Threw up some more.

   I wonder if Mom knows what it's like to swallow someone else's snot, someone else's spit.

Ms. Perfect—wonder how perfect she'd be if she swallowed some snot. Sucked down some spit—puked *her* brains out.

I'm sick of it.

I'm sick of all this *shit*.

My insides are starting to seep through. My hell, trying to get to the surface, ripping up my guts on its way to the top.

I need to see Mr. Tanner. He'll know what to do . . . He'll get me straight . . .

Just have to keep it together. Just a little while longer, just have to keep my self

to
ge
t
h
e
r.

Halfway

through fifth-period Spanish, and I'm starting to feel
angry. I'm starting to feel guilty. I'm starting to feel *hungry. Tengo hambre.*
Lunch is next, and my stomach is rumbling. Everything's
gettin' all jumbled in my head.

"Probably cause you have low blood sugar." That's
what Mom would say. She's always like: "Tisha, you need
to eat. You're feeling like this because you have low blood
sugar." That's her answer to everything, low blood sugar.
I need to eat? My booty is too big as it is. Tiny says it's
not, but come on. I love Tiny and everything, but her
booty's got its own area code. She said that to me once
and we both fell out laughing. Every time I saw her that
day, I'd look at her booty and we'd both double over,
laughing and carrying on.

I haven't told Tiny about what Beth said. I wanted to,
but I just couldn't. I know she would want revenge. I
know she's planning somethin' for Cheryl and Vicky. She
told me that by the time she's done with them, they'll
never mess with us again. I'm not sure what she's got
planned. I know she's got a cousin who's kind of shady,

been in and out of juvenile jail. I hope she's not gonna' get *him* involved. You never know with Tiny. She can surprise you sometimes.

"You shouldn't sink to their level." That's what Mom tells me, but maybe you *have* to sink, maybe just a little . . . I should sink to their level long enough to kick their butts; that's what I should do.

The smell of greasy fries is makin' me crazy. That's what you get for having class next to the cafeteria. I think they're servin' double dogs and country beans today. They're not the best hot dogs I've ever tasted, but when you're real hungry they're good enough. And today, I could eat just about anything.

"I am staaahvin like Maaahvin," Tiny whispers in my ear. Well, not exactly a whisper, she sounds like she's talking through a microphone, and at close range, ooouch!

"I'm staaahvin, too." I whisper back.

"Hey, Tisha, where's your boyfriend?" Tiny points to Kurt's empty chair.

"How should I know?" I snap back at Tiny.

"Oh yeah, you like him alright. It's written all over your face . . ."

"Whatever." I try to say it like I could care less, but I'm not foolin' Tiny. I'm not even foolin' myself . . .

Seniors rule!

"Duncan, you're late."

"Sorry, Mr. Novak, had a previous engagement."

Spontaneous laughter from the class.

"This is becoming a pattern, Mr. Duncan. The fact that you're a football player does not afford you any special treatment in my class. You cannot just waltz in here whenever you please and expect there to be no repercussions. Now, if my calculations are correct, you only have thirty minutes in which to complete the test. No extra time, no retests. Now, have a seat."

"That's about twenty-five minutes more than I need . . . for your easy tests,"
Ryan says under his breath, but just loud enough for Mr. Novak and most of the class to hear. The class breaks out into a spontaneous hushed OOOOOH.

"You're really slipping, Mr. Duncan, such a shame. I remember when you used to be smart."
A louder spontaneous OOOOOH from the class.

"You know what? I don't even have to take this test. I'm automatically graduating. I've got enough credits and you know it. There's nothing you can do about it, either."
The class is silent. They look shocked at what Ryan said.

"Get out of here, Mr. Duncan. Go see Principal Roberts. He'll be expecting you. I'm going to give him a call, get him up to speed on the little scene you caused today. You two should have a very nice chat. I'm sure he'd be glad to enlighten you as to the finer points of the school handbook. Suffice it to say, in this school, as in life, there are no guarantees."

"Yeah, whatever. Me and Roberts go way back. I would love to see him.

"Seniors rule! BEARS for life!!"

Ryan slams the classroom door. Smiling to himself, walking briskly toward Principal Roberts's office.

Rockville High Times
Issues of our time

GUN CONTROL

Hold it in your hands; don't shake.
Steady now.
Carefully line up your target.
Gently squeeze the trigger.

(Repeat if necessary.)

Hiding out

It's almost lunch and I finally peeled myself off the toilet. My face under the faucet now. The cold water feels good. I swallow some, but most of it I spit out. My mouth still tastes of vomit, but it's not as bad as it was. Found a couple of mints in my backpack; that helped some.

My legs are stiff from having them propped up on the toilet for so long.

It feels like time just stopped, like I'm in this other world. Have to see Mr. T before lunch. I know he goes home for lunch, he lives right down the street from school.

Mr. Tanner has a little boy, Tommy. He always tells me what Tommy's been doing. How he's just starting to say words, and just beginning to walk, stuff like that. Mr. Tanner's the only one who I can talk to. It's more like he's the only one who will listen. Nobody else listens to me. He really wants to know about me. He wants to know who I am. He listens like he cares. Like he really wants me to feel better, feel better about myself. I want to, but I don't know if I ever will. I'd never tell Mr. T that. He's always so positive. He makes me positive, too. At least for a little while . . . Then it comes back. It always comes back . . .

OW, got a cramp. I gotta get out of here. Smells like puke and shit in here. I'll be all right. I just have to see Mr. T. Mr. Tanner will know what to do.

He'll know . . .

I'm sure of it.

The note

slipped ever so gently into her locker. Just enough room to slide it through. God bless the American Locker Corporation.

I would be derelict in my duty if I didn't at least try, don't you think? It is a busy day, but there's always time for a beautiful lady. I know what you're thinking: you're thinking that I, Floater, don't have a chance in hell with this girl. Well, I beg to differ. I only made one attempt, and that was really just akin to welcoming a new neighbor with an apple pie. That was just my opening volley, if you will. Just a shot across the bow . . .

Put it down on paper, that's what I always say. Words just evaporate into air, but when you write them down, they have *power, meaning.*

Tisha seems like the kind of girl who responds to the written word. Well, I think she's gonna like what she reads. She's going to like it *a lot . . .*

chapter 10

Part 1
The Charge

Ryan: Look, Mr. Roberts. I don't know what Mr. Novak's so mad about, but I'll apologize if you want me to. I just got a little carried away, what with the game and everything tonight. You know, I'm a senior. It's kind of our privilege to get a little crazy, isn't it?

Roberts: I couldn't agree with you more, but that's not what I want to talk to you about. I was going to call you down, after lunch, but since you're here . . . Well, this is really hard for me to say . . . So I guess I'll just come out and say it.

Ryan: What?

Roberts: I got a call last night, at my home, from a Peggy McConnell. I believe you know her daughter, Kimberly?

Ryan: Yeah, I know Kim.

Roberts: Well, ah, hmm, Mrs. McConnell says that you made unwanted sexual advances toward her daughter last week.

Ryan: What—?

Roberts: Her mother states that last Friday you took Kimberly into the girls' locker room and started touching her inappropriately. Mrs. McConnell says that Kimberly resisted and repeatedly told you to stop. When you didn't stop, she tried to break away from you, but you forced her to stay by holding her arms down.

Ryan: Get the f——

Roberts: Her mother went on to tell me that Kimberly finally was able to break free after your pager went off and you were distracted for a minute.

Ryan: You have *got* to be kidding me. No way . . . unwanted? She was all over *me*. I think it was *definitely* wanted. Besides, nothing happened anyway.
I really wasn't interested . . . This is just a big misunderstanding. I can straighten this whole thing out. Trust me, Mr. Roberts, I can . . .

LUNCH!

Skinny kid who hates the cafeteria food: You see this slop? This is what you should be talking about on the news. They serve better stuff in prisons. I mean, would you eat it?

Mandy Montgomery: Well, I don't exactly have a choice do I? I'm stuck here for the rest of the day. Now, let's get back to *why* I'm here. Jake Stiles? The one-year anniversary of his death? Have you seen a change in the students here at Rockville? A change in how they are relating towards one another? Maybe you've even experienced it yourself? I guess what I'm trying to get at is: in your opinion, is what we're seeing now a kinder, gentler Rockville High?

SKWHTCF: Now, *these* are supposed to be hot dogs. Do these things look like hot dogs to you? Do they even resemble anything in the processed-food family? I think not. I think, next time instead of bringing your cameraman, you should bring the health inspector down here. I mean you want an exclusive—this *cole slaw* is an exclusive . . .

MM: BOBBY! LUNCH! And could you run over to Hamburger Halo? I'm not touchin' this stuff . . .

You never see the shit until it hits the fan . . .

Part 2
The Defense

Roberts: Look, Ryan, I've known you for a long time, but this thing here, this is bad. This is real bad. Quite frankly, I was shocked when I got the call. Mrs. McConnell was extremely upset. I mean, she went ballistic. I have to tell you, she was very convincing.

I want to give you a chance now, Ryan. A chance to tell

me your side of the story. This is your chance to set the record straight.

Ryan: It's like I said. She was all over me. It started out with Kim flirting with me like *crazy* before study hall. Then she was like, let's go somewhere where we can be alone. I was like, okay. So I found an out-of-the-way spot, but once we got there, I really lost interest. She was kind of coming on too strong, if you know what I mean.

Roberts: So what you're saying is that nothing happened?

Ryan: That's exactly what I'm saying. Nothing happened.

Roberts: Kim is lying then?

Ryan: I guess she must be. Either her or her mom. Somebody's lying 'cause nothing happened. Look, why don't we just bring Kim down here. I think we could clear up this whole thing before lunch is over.

Roberts: I wish it was that easy. Things are a bit more complicated now.

Ryan: What do you mean? Complicated . . . ?

Roberts: Well, for one thing, Kimberly's not here.

Ryan: Yeah, she is. I saw her this morning.

Roberts: Well, she was here, but she's not now. Her mother pulled her out of school right before lunch. She was worried about her safety—after you found out about all of this.

Ryan: Her safety? What kind of person does she think I am? Kim is cool. I don't have anything against her. She's probably just mad 'cause I wouldn't return *her* advances. I mean, truth be told, Mr. Roberts, she was the one who made unwanted sexual advances toward *me*. I mean, *I'm* the one who should be accusing *her*. Come on, Mr. Roberts, you're a very reasonable man. We go way back. Now, who are you going to believe? Me, Ryan Duncan, an all-American quarterback with an unblemished school record, or some wannabe freshman girl with an ax to grind? No disrespect to Kim, but it's obvious, isn't it? I think we both know who's lying here, don't we?

Another blow . . . for Kurt

"Mr. Tanner just left.Oh,well,is he coming back later?Oh,okay.IsTommy alright?Oh,it's okay.No,it's okay,it's not an emergency.No,don't page him.It's okay.Everything's cool.
Yeah,I'm sure,I'm fine.
Thanks."

The kid, Kurt, is standing in front of his locker. Students whiz by at breakneck speeds, bouncing about in every direction, most of them racing to lunch.

Opening his locker, Kurt rummages around for a few seconds. His back is to me. I can't see exactly what he's doing. I am a safe distance away. Someone darts by and slaps him on the back of the neck. Kurt doesn't even flinch. I see him bending down on one knee. He appears to be unzipping something inside his locker. It looks like a bag, but his body is blocking me, keeping me from getting a closer look. He turns towards me, just for a moment. I step back into the throng of kids, camouflaging myself for a second. I walk closer to Kurt, taking the long way around to his locker, making sure he doesn't see me. Getting close now, I can almost make out his expression. His eyes seem to light up as he stares into the bag. It appears to be a gym bag. A crooked smile scribbles itself across his face. Kurt quickly erases it with a twitch of his lips.

Another student runs past and slaps him on the back of the neck. A red welt slowly begins to form. Kurt stands up and quickly slams his locker shut. I duck back into another row of lockers and watch him. He is carrying a medium-sized blue-and-gray gym bag as he walks quickly away.

Kurt joins the rest of the herd heading for lunch. I follow. I see him stop suddenly and take a long look back towards his locker. For a moment he seems unsure of himself.

He continues toward the cafeteria. I let him go, watching him slowly disappear into the crowd.

You never see the shit until it hits the fan . . .

Part 3
The Sentence

Roberts: I'm going to be honest with you, Ryan. I'm not really sure *who* to believe. One thing I am sure of is that Mrs. McConnell is not going to let this thing go. She's really holding my feet to the fire on this. She's threatening legal action; she's threatening to talk to the media. This thing could really get ugly, Ryan—for both of us.

Ryan: What are you saying?

Roberts: What I'm saying is that I'm going to have to take some kind of action. And I'm going to have to act fast. I'm sorry, Ryan. This is just a real bad day. It's the one-year anniversary of a student being murdered and I've got a news crew roaming around the school, asking students God knows what. I can't let this thing get out of hand, especially not today.

Ryan: I'm not really sure where this is going, Mr. Roberts. What type of action are you talking about? I mean, it is clear to you that Kim is lying, isn't it?

Roberts: Nothing is clear, son; that's the problem. It's basically her word against yours. I'm sorry, Ryan, but I'm going to have to suspend you pending further investigation into this matter.

Ryan: Suspend me? *Whoa*, wait up a minute. Okay. Let's not jump off the deep end here. I know you've got to take some action, but don't you think that's a little extreme? What about a hearing? I know I get a hearing. I can totally clear myself at a school hearing.

Roberts: We've got a zero tolerance policy, Ryan. It is my opinion that this alleged sexual assault falls well within that policy. The policy requires me to give you an automatic five-day suspension, effective at the end of the school day today.

There's something else, too. You cannot participate in any extracurricular activities whatsoever for the duration of the suspension.

I'm sorry, Ryan, you can't play tonight.

Ryan: What? Now it's sexual assault? I can't play tonight? Do you hear what you're saying? Do you know what this means? This is my future we're talking about. It's the playoffs tonight. I've got scouts coming to this game. I mean, I've been offered a scholarship, but it's conditional. They can take it away from me. And don't think they won't. They want to see me with the pressure on. We're going for our third Championship in a row this year. This is a huge game tonight. How is that going to look, the top quarterback in the state missing the first round of the playoffs because he's been suspended? And the reason for the suspension is *sexual assault*. Oh, that's going to sit real well with the coaches over at U. State. You can't do this to me, Roberts, you can't.

Roberts: Look, it's out of my hands. I have to give you the suspension.

Ryan: That's bullshit. You don't *have to* do anything; you're the principal.

Roberts: I know you're upset, but you need to watch the language.

Ryan: Okay, I'm sorry. Look, if you have to suspend me, why don't you just do it after the game tonight? Mrs. McConnell gets what she wants and I get what I want.

Roberts: I'm sorry, Ryan, it just doesn't work like that. My decision is final. You're suspended effective three-fifteen today. You will have a chance to defend yourself in front of the school disciplinary board. A hearing date will be set on Monday.

Ryan: You know, you're a real piece of work. Always looking to save your own ass. I should have known you'd screw me. You know, I'm not going to let you get away with this.

Roberts: I think you'd best get on to lunch, cool off a bit. If you want to talk about it some more, after you cool off, you can come down and see me. I'm sorry, Ryan, but I just don't have a choice. I think you should really take a good hard look at yourself, son. Obviously *something* happened to make Mrs. McConnell so upset. You know if you play with fire, one day you're gonna get burned.

Ryan: Spare me your country wisdom, *please*. You know the Colonel is *not* going to like this. Have you thought about that, you stupid—

Roberts: I think you should leave now. You really don't want to make things harder on yourself. Trust me, you don't . . .

chapter 11

Sixth-period lunch. I sit with Tiny and some other girls. I guess you could call us the misfits. We're the ones who don't fit in. I heard some girls call us the loser table, but me and Tiny know we're not losers.

We like *misfits*. Fits us just right.

I can't understand a word Tiny is saying. She loves to talk with her mouth full. And she talks fast, too. Faster with her mouth full than when it's not. Tiny loves to gossip. French fries go in and gossip comes out. She's tellin' me about how some boy I don't even know is havin' sex with some girl I don't even know. I don't think Tiny knows them, either, but she'll still tell you about it like she's the girl's best friend or somethin'. Typical Tiny gossip. She is *such* a trip. She just goes on and on. When she's on a gossip binge? You'd better watch out. I'm only half listening anyway. I am in double-dog heaven. I'm in mid-bite when I finally look up, kind of nod at Tiny like I've been following what she's been sayin'. She could be sayin' that space aliens are coming to invade the school, and I wouldn't know it.

Country beans aren't as good today, but I'm eating them anyway. Mom's are way better, but I am staaahvin— there's Kurt, standing about four tables away, in the middle of the cafeteria. He's looking for somewhere to sit.

I guess I do kinda like him. I mean, he is cute in a real shy kinda way.

Shy, like me.

I kind of feel bad for him, too. I know he has a hard time.
He gets picked on a lot. Maybe I like him 'cause I feel
sorry for him.
I don't know . . . He always seems alright, acts like
nothin's really bothering him. He's probably just a good
actor. That's what you have to be in high school,
a good actor.
I should just walk over there, invite him to sit with us.
Tiny would never let me hear the end of that. But why do
I care what Tiny thinks all the time?
Shoot, now I lost him . . .
I wish they were servin' *Mom's* country beans.
Yeah, her beans are waaaaay better . . .

Ryan's long walk

Lunchtime and my mind is racing.
I am *so* fucked.
I can't believe this shit. This can't be happening. Susie's
gonna lose it when she finds out.
And she *will* find out. Kim is such a bitch. What the hell
did I ever do to her?
I mean, she wanted me as much as I wanted her.
Unwanted sexual advances?
That's her mom, trying to nail me.
I knew Kim was upset, but I didn't think she was so upset
she'd tell her mom.

   If Kim was in school, I know she would listen to me. I
know I could get her to talk to her mom and stop all this

madness. So I got a little carried away? Kim wasn't complaining when she had her tongue halfway down my throat. I guess that was okay.

How am I supposed to stop my play once the ball is snapped?

Fuckin' Roberts. School policy, my ass. He knows he can get around that shit. I've seen him do it. Playin' me for a punk, that's what he's doing. I'm not gonna let him get away with this. I'm gonna beat it. Just have to figure out how.

We were supposed to be tight. Bastard. And the Colonel, that's a whole other freak show. I can't even think about that. All I know is *I am* playing tonight, and I'm *not* gonna lose Susie over some bullshit like this.

I just have to stay calm, like I'm in a game. Fourth down, and we have to score a touchdown—Win or go home.

Win

or go

home.

I always feel better

when I have my gym bag with me. I thought I'd try to make it the whole day without it—I might have been able to if Tanner had been in. Doesn't matter, I'm okay. Things will be okay . . . I'm in control; I'm in control now . . .

I'm *so* hungry, but today is the day. I am really going to start my diet today. I'll even go one better: I'm not going to eat at all today. It will be a testament to my love for her. Love, well, that was a little strong. Let me restate that. I am in *serious like,* how's that?

I can do it, I mean, not eat. I've done it before, well, not on purpose, but it did happen once. Back before I had my business, back when I had negative cash flow. I've never actually not eaten on purpose, but this, this is different, this is *serious like.*

I've got a mirror, I know what I'm up against, but it can be done. I can turn it around; it's not too late. I've *got* to look good for Tisha—mmmmm . . .

I hope she reads my note before the end of the day. She'll probably write me back. Telling me how much she admires *me.* How much she'd like to get to know *me* better. Oh, the wording might be slightly different, but she'll respond in kind. I know she will. She'll probably slip a note into *my* locker. I can't wait.

Oh, the anticipation is killing me . . .

Greasy Chatter
Big Brother . . .

"Dude, this is like the tenth time they've served these dogs. I am so sick of 'em."

"Me too, but I'm starvin'."

"It's crazy seein' so much security on campus, reminds me of last year."

"I know, they were all up in my shit, too. Lookin' over my shoulder when I was opening my locker. Can they do that?"

"Dude, they can do whatever they want. Didn't you read *1984* in Mrs. Grant's English lit? Dude, it's Big Brother. No such thing as privacy anymore."

"Dude, I don't know *what* you're talking about . . ."

"You know George Orwell, *1984*?"

"I must have been absent that day."

"Dude, you're absent even when you're here."

"Damn, that's fucked up."

"It's true."

"I know."

slow motion . . .

I feel like I'm in slow motion, walking to her table. I know I'm moving forward, but it's taking so long . . .

There she is, my sweet Susie Sunshine talking to Beth.
She sees me coming but she's not smiling.
She knows; she already knows. If *she* knows, it must be
all over school. I bet everyone knew before I did.

I wish it was like before, like this morning—everything
was fine. I wish I could just rewind to this morning, first
period.

Moving so slow—motion to her table.
So slow . . .
It feels like I'll *never* get there.

I hope I don't.

Technical difficulties

Russ in the studio: Let's go live now, to Mandy
Montgomery at Rockville High, where she's been inter-
viewing students all morning for her exclusive report **Are
the Kids really alright?**
Mandy . . . ?

(Long pause)

Russ: Mandy? Are you there? Mandy? . . .
Okay. We're having some technical difficulties with our
mobile hookup. We'll get that straightened out as soon as
we can.

Let's go to a commercial.
We'll be right back with what we hope is a live report
from Mandy Montgomery.

Now, for this important commercial message

Voice of commercial announcer: Are your kids just too
much for you? Are they constantly getting into trouble
around the house? Always playing their music too loud?
Is the unending disrespect and teenage rebellion wearing
you down? Then it's time to get **NumbedOut**.
NumbedOut is a safe and effective way of completely
tuning out your children. Just take two tablets fifteen
minutes before they come home from school, and you're
on your way to a peaceful and stress-free evening.

    NumbedOut works as a filter. Filtering out your kids
from your consciousness, but leaving your spouse and
household pets for you to enjoy. **NumbedOut** is all
natural and there are absolutely no side effects. None,
whatsoever.

NumbedOut is the safe and adult way to deal with those
unruly youngsters.
So the next time your child says:

    "F*** you, Mom" *(girl says to mom)* or
    "F*** you, Dad" *(boy says to dad)*
get **NumbedOut** and forget they were ever born . . .

*Voice of different commercial announcer reading
extremely fast:*

NumbedOut and its parent company, Control Substances, not responsible for lost, missing, or runaway children. **NumbedOut** not for parents already indifferent to or uninterested in their children, since the effect will be enhanced greatly by the taking of this drug. Do not operate heavy machinery or read anything over three and a half pages long for at least eight hours after last dose.

Live from a lunchroom near you . . .

(The kids are definitely *not* alright . . .)

Mandy Montgomery: This is Mandy Montgomery live at Rockville High, where I've been conducting interviews for my exclusive report,
Are the Kids really alright?
I've got a student here, a Noreen Goodall, who was just sharing with me some very interesting thoughts.

MM: Noreen, let me just come out and ask you, do you think the kids are really alright? Or have we lost our children?

NG: I think the kids are fu**** up. Oh sorry, I hope you can bleep that out.

MM: I'm not sure if they caught that in time; please remember we are *live*.

NG: Oh, sorry. What I mean is that I think there are a lot of kids who just don't care anymore. For whatever reason, they've had it, and they really don't think about the consequences of their actions.

MM: Do you know any of these kids personally?

NG: I know of them.

MM: These kids that you know of, how many of them do you think are capable of violence? Particularly violence towards their fellow students or teachers?

NG: I'd have to say, a lot of them. I've heard things, sometimes right from the kids themselves. I'm tellin' you it's just a matter of time before we have another shooting, and the next time it could be a lot worse.

MM: Well, Russ, there you have it, straight from the mouth of Noreen Goodall, a senior here at Rockville High. You can see the rest of my interviews tonight and every night next week, in my exclusive 7 Alive report **Are the Kids really alright?**

Lunchtime vigil

"Tiny, how come they're havin' this in the cafeteria?"

"I guess they figured people would already be here, eatin'."

"These kids are so rude. They're just stuffin' their faces, like they don't even care."

"Let us pray.
We thank you, Father, for letting us know Jacob Stiles.
Even if it was just for a short time, you gave us a kind human being, with a good soul.
Although his life met a violent end, Jacob did not live a life of violence. He lived a life of peace, helping those who needed help, being a good friend, a good son, a good citizen of this—"

"Tisha, who is Reverend McNeely talkin' about? Jake was a wannabe gangster who got in *way* over his head. Everybody knows that."

"Well, maybe the Reverend knew Jake. I mean, I didn't really know him, but he seemed nice. I mean, maybe he did some bad stuff, but that doesn't make him *all* bad. He definitely didn't deserve to end up like that . . ."

"I know he didn't deserve to *die,* but you gotta get a grip, Tisha. Jake was a bad dude. Sometimes you are so naive."

"Guess I just like to believe there's some good in everyone . . ."

"Well, I guess he didn't have enough good in him to steer clear of trouble. What he needed was some *good* sense; that's what he needed. Come on, the bell's gonna ring soon. They're gonna be here for a while. We got to get to class."

"Wait a minute, Tiny. It's nice what he's sayin'. Makes me feel good.

"He can't be just makin' stuff up. A man of God doesn't lie. Does he?"

Susie's storm

Now Beth sees me, too. She waits until I sit down, then gets up from the table.
She brushes past me without saying a word.

Cue the thunder and lightning:

"When were you going to tell me, Ryan? Huh? Were you going to wait until it was on the six o'clock news? How could you do this to me? After everything we've been through together. I stayed by your side; I always stayed by your side."

"You have to believe me, babe. It's bullshit . . . it's not true. Kim is lying. She's got it in for me. You have to believe me."

"Kim? Who the hell is Kim? I'm talking about Becky Boswell. Beth just told me she saw you having sex with Becky in the girls' locker room yesterday. I thought that was *our special* place. Is that where you take all your *other* girls, too? I didn't even know about this *Kim*. Thanks for the update. What are you trying to go for, some kind of record or something? You're unbelievable. I thought you loved me, Ryan? You said you loved me . . ."

"Wait, Susie. Don't cry. Come back. Don't leave mad like this—you have to hear my side of it. Susie, Susie . . . I can fix this . . ."

"How can you fix this? You've been with at least two other girls, and those are just the ones I know of. Do you know how horrible that is? How horrible it makes me feel? Not to mention how it makes me look?

"Like I'm a doormat for you to walk all over whenever you want?

"I've never, *ever* been so disrespected in my life.

"How could you do this to me? To us? You ruined everything, Ryan. You ruined everything . . . *my* life, *our* life, everything . . .

"You can't fix this, Ryan, not this time."

Tears are streaming down her face as she walks away.
Everyone is heading out of the lunchroom, getting ready for seventh period.
I just sit. Paralyzed.
*I lay my head on the table and close my eyes. Maybe this is just a really bad dream and when I open my eyes everything will be alright—everything will be like it was . . . I shut my eyes tighter—trying to keep out reality . . . trying to close out the world. This isn't happening, this is **not** happening . . .*

chapter 12

Random kid #1: Hey, Dirt, you planning on workin' out? You know you could use it . . . Maybe you can answer me this question. How come you always got that gym bag with you, but you never seem to get any muscles?

Random kid #2: Maybe he's just not lifting enough weight?

RK #1: Yeah, that's probably it. Hey, Dirt, how much can you bench? Huh, what are you up to now? Somethin' like ten, fifteen pounds . . . ?

RK #2: No, I think it's more like five. Look at those arms, man. My little sister's got more muscle than he does.

RK #1: Damn, you hear that, Dirt? Are you going to just sit there and take that? Man, he's calling you a little girl. Are you a little girl?

RK #2: Yeah, he's a little girl. Look at him. He won't even say anything back. What a pussy.

RK #1: Damn, did you hear that? Now he's calling you a pussy. Are you a pussy, Dirt?

Their words are like a hand smacking me in the face. Where's Mr. Shoemaker? Couldn't he be on time to algebra just once?

Damn, I suck—always looking for someone to save me. I don't turn around. I'm pretending I'm writing something important. I wish I had my greatest hits notebook. Left it in my backpack in my locker. Mr. Tanner says it's good to write stuff down. Says it's a release. I guess it helps sometimes, but not now.

No, now is shit. I can't keep up with my pile; I can't keep up. As much as I try, more gets dumped on top of me. Bag after bag of trash poured over my head. How much garbage can a person live in? Does Mr. T really expect me to live my life this way? Forever? Always being dumped on? No, he can't expect me to keep taking this, can he? These morons have no idea. Nobody does, not even Mr. T. They have no idea who I really am, what I'm really capable of. Yeah, I'll sit and take it, but my pile is almost to the top now. There's no more room. Do they know what that means? I don't think so. No one does, not even Mr. T. They don't know that I have the power right here, right in my hands. Well, maybe it's time for me to show my power. Maybe I should say something back, but when I talk, when I finally say something, it won't be with words . . . These fools will hear me alright; everyone will hear me. Then they'll wonder why they treated me this way. They'll wish they had just tried to talk to me, talk to me like I was a person—treated me like a *real* person, not just a punching bag, not just a big garbage can to throw shit into, to piss on. They'll wish they could take it all back, but they won't be able to. It'll be too late. Yeah, I've got something to say . . . You wanna hear it? Huh? Do you *really* want to?

(Hail Mary)

Coach Larry Johnson: Hey, Ron, got a minute?

Principal Roberts: Sure, Larry, have a seat.

The Coach: I just left Ryan Duncan a few minutes ago. The kid was practically in tears. I mean this thing, Ron, this is bad. He's got scouts coming tonight. Ron, this could really ruin the kid. I really wish I'd been called in on this. I mean, maybe we could have worked a way around this. What I'm trying to say is, I think you should reconsider your decision here. I believe the kid. I think this Kim girl made the whole thing up. She did wait a whole week before she told anybody.

Roberts: Larry, I understand where you're coming from. I know you've invested a lot in Duncan, but my hands are tied. It's school policy. Zero tolerance means zero tolerance. There's a lot at stake here, Larry. I've got to think about what's in the best interests of the school, too. This affects all of us, you know.

The Coach: I can appreciate the spot this puts you in. All I'm saying is maybe there's another way. Maybe we could call in this McConnell woman, sit down, and talk. Get Duncan and the girl in here, too. I think if we get everyone together, we can get this thing over with, and quick.

In the end, that's what you want, isn't it, Ron? We can resolve this before it has to go any further.

Roberts: I wish we could, Larry, but you didn't hear that woman screaming at me on the phone. The last thing I need is to have her here at the school, angry and upset, with access to that news reporter we've got roaming the halls. That is a recipe for disaster, if you ask me.

The Coach: Look, Ron, you're really not giving me much to work with here. The kid is an all-American. *An all-American.* He's been offered a four-year scholarship to U. State, and he's one of the first kids I've had that could be a college star. Ron, I've had college coaches tell me he's pro material. *Pro material,* Ron. There has got to be another way. I mean, come on, let the kid play tonight. Then if you have to take action at least it will be after the game. The suspension would be over before the second round. See, Ron, if you just work with me on this there's a way we can make it come out okay. U. State never has to know. We can keep it off his transcripts.

Roberts: You're not asking me to—

The Coach: You've bent the rules in the past, Ron. We've both been in some bad spots, some worse than this, and we've managed to work it out. Together, Ron, remember?

Roberts: I remember, and you should remember that I've taken care of more than a few problems for you. You don't exactly have a team full of angels. Larry, we're friends. We were friends before this; we'll be friends after. I just can't do it this time. This time we're going to have to ride it out. I'm sorry, Larry, but there's nothing I can do.

The Coach: I think you can do something, Ron, you just don't want to. You're scared. You've always been scared. If we're both being honest here, let's *really* get honest. You want to save your own hide. That's what this is all about. This isn't so much about protecting the school as it is about *saving your ass*.

Roberts: Okay. Watch it, now.

The Coach: Watch what? I just can't sit here and let this kid's life go down the drain. I've got to do something. I'm going to make some calls. This isn't over, Ron. This is not over.

Tisha takes a stand

"We're late," I shout back to Tiny.

"I know," Tiny yells up to me, sounding out of breath. Racing to seventh-period Computer Soft—I feel my shoe getting stepped on. Cheryl laughs as she walks past me.

"What are you laughin' at?" The words fly out of my mouth before I can put them back in. Cheryl stops dead in her tracks and turns around.

"What? Did you say something, Half N Half?"

"Don't call me that." Tiny is with me now, hearing what is going on. I get bolder as Tiny comes to my side. It's two on one now. Just Cheryl against Me and Tiny. Cheryl doesn't back down. She gets right in my face. Her hate and nasty breath make me want to turn away, but I don't. Not this time.

"Don't call me that," I say again. "That's not my name. My name is Tisha Reznick. Okay?"

"Step away from my girl, or you're gonna get two hundred and fifty pounds of hurt crashin' down on your thick head," Tiny says, getting up in Cheryl's face. Cheryl looks unsure. For the first time, she almost looks scared. She looks around for her girl, Vicky, but she's not there.

"You're lucky my girl's not here or you two would get busted up real good." Now *I* get up in Cheryl's face. Sometimes bravery is contagious.

"You're not gonna bust up anybody. You're not gonna mess with us again, you understand? We know people, and you don't want to mess with them." My threat catches Tiny off guard. A look of surprise opens up across her face. Tiny lets out a "You go, girl" as she nods her head. It catches Cheryl off guard, too.

"You two don't know anybody. You just talkin' shit." The quiver in Cheryl's voice makes it sound like she doesn't totally believe what she's saying.

"You listen here," Tiny says, back in her face. "You tell your girl, Vicky, that my cousin Eddie Edwards and his *friend* Trent will be in your ass if you ever mess with either one of us again. *Com-pren-de?*"
Tiny drags out the *comprende* real long, almost spitting the word into Cheryl's face. Kids are flyin' by. Most don't

even notice what's going on. A couple of kids are watching off to the side.

"Let's go. We're really late now," Tiny says under her breath.

We bump our chests into Cheryl as we go by her. I look over my shoulder and Cheryl's still standing there, like she's still talking to us. She looks ridiculous.

I guess she always did.

I get my pass and I'm gone . . .

My head hurts. I feel like there's an army of soldiers with sledgehammers pounding away at my brain. I can't hear anything Mr. Shoemaker is saying.

Just pounding in my head.

"Kurt, you alright?" Phil whispers just loud enough so I can hear.

I don't answer.

I gotta get outta here. My hand goes up, the stares shoot back.

I get my pass and I'm gone . . .

Feeling the pressure
7th period

I feel like all eyes are on me. I'm used to it out on the field, but not like this. Whispers travel from seat to seat, desk to desk. Girls shooting daggers with their stares—

friends of Susie, other girls, too. Everyone piling on, like a sack. Everyone sacking the quarterback.

I can't believe this shit. Roberts is not going to get away with this. I can get out of it. I know I can. I just need to figure out how. I have to get in touch with Kim. I should just call over there right now. That's what I should do—no, her mom will probably answer and then I'd never be able to talk her.

"Is it true?" Stew looks at me in disbelief. Saying those three words like his life depended on it. Like my life depended on it.

"Don't worry, dude, I'm going to get out of it. I'll play tonight." Stew looks satisfied with my answer. I wish I was.

I know Coach Johnson is trying to help. Maybe he can get the alumni to put some pressure on Roberts. I think that's what he said he was going to do. I hope he doesn't call the Colonel. I told him not to. I don't know, he might be my best chance. The Colonel can definitely get things done. Maybe I should—

"Dude, what's going on? I heard you got suspended. You're still playin' tonight, right?" Zak's face is as serious as I've ever seen it.

"It's cool. I'm gonna play. I'd have to be in a coma not to play tonight. Roberts will back down if he knows what's good for him."

Zak tries to smile, but he doesn't seem convinced.

"Dude, they can't do this shit to you. No way. No way

are they gonna stop you from playin' tonight. No way."
Zak starts to get loud.

"Dude, it's cool. It's gonna be alright." I try to calm
him. Once Zak gets riled up, forget it. Last thing I need is
to get kicked out of class. Everybody just needs to chill—
okay, take a deep breath and try to think . . .
think . . .

Floater's find

This locker could use some tidying up. Looks like a hurri-
cane hit this thing. Ah, here it is. So predictable . . . bottom
of the backpack inside another book. *mY Greatest hiTs*.
This is it. I bet you never thought this would fall into the
wrong hands, did ya, sucker? They just don't guard locker
combinations like they used to. Too easy to hack into sys-
tems these days. *Thank you, geek squad.* Damn, this kid is
twisted. Maybe not twisted enough for Roberts, though. I
may need to do some creative writing here. Where are all
the kids' names? He calls this a hit list? This is not going to
fly as is. If Roberts wants a hit list, I'll give him a *hit list* . . .

The thrill of victory . . .

"Sophomore power!"

"That felt so good, Tiny. I feel like I just jumped out of
a plane or something."

"I know. I feel good, too."

"Did you see the look on Cheryl's face? I think she was scared. She was scared of *us*, can you believe it?"

"I don't know about all that. She might've been scared, but I don't think it was of us. She was scared of my cousin and Trent. Those boys have a reputation. Everybody heard of them."

"It doesn't matter. She was still scared. You were awesome, Tiny! I thought you might push her down right then and there."

"I was thinkin' hard about it, but I didn't want to get busted. Hey, T, you weren't too bad yourself, gettin' all up in Cheryl's face. You my girl."

"Just tryin' to be like you, Tiny. That's all."

"Did you study for the quiz, T?"

"Yeah, how 'bout you?"

"We better be quiet; Mr. Jenkins just shot me a look."

"We'll talk in eighth period?"

"Not gonna be there, T. I have a doctor's appointment."

"Dag, Tiny, I was looking forward to cuttin' up with

you in study hall. You're still comin' out to eat tonight, right?"

"Wouldn't miss it. Is your dad comin', too?"

"No, he's out of town on business. It'll just be my mom and us."

"Cool."

A Floater freight train . . . (An unstoppable force)

Stomach rumbling, sneakers squeaking, pants swooshing. A Floater freight train rolling down the halls to Roberts's office. An unstoppable force. Unstoppable. I guess I'm not the most inconspicuous person in the school right now. I don't care. I'm on a mission. And soon that mission will be accomplished. I don't care if you can hear me coming from a mile away. The fact is that I'm coming, and I'm about to pull off one of the great moves of my career. Now, that is saying something. I've had quite an illustrious career, but this, this is going to be in the top ten. This is definitely going to make the highlight reel. This is it right here—this notebook that I'm cradling like a baby. This notebook is my golden opportunity. After I pull this off, I will leapfrog over Roberts into the category of the untouchables. I will be in the hall of fame. I will go down as one of the best operators in history. And this operation is foolproof. That means even Roberts can't mess it up.

Oh, it's going to work. It's definitely going to work. It all fits. It all makes sense. You know why? Because I made it make sense. I just needed to take a little poetic license with his work. Kurt needed a little editorial assistance. Well, actually he needed a lot. His stuff didn't have enough edge. You know what I mean? He was headed in the right direction, but his hit list needed to be more dramatic. The kid lacked imagination. Hey, if there's one thing I have, it's *imagination*. When Roberts gets a look at this, Kurt will be out of this school so fast, his head will spin. Do I feel bad about it? Not really. He's just a casualty of war. Collateral damage. The kid would pop eventually. I'm just taking a pre-emptive strike. Oh, it's hard to be me sometimes. Well, not really, I love it. Look at the alternative. All these schnooks sitting in class. Don't they know it's not going to help them in the real world? **This** is the real world. I am the real world. I should be teaching here. Teach these kids what they need to know to get ahead, what they need to know to make some real money. Yeah, I could teach them a thing or two . . .

Ah, I've arrived.

Yes, I have.

The past coming back

I just have to think . . . But I don't like what's coming into my head. Instead of the future, I'm thinking about the past. The Colonel. My mom. I have to stay focused. Keep my mind on *this* hell. **One** hell at a time. What the fuck am I gonna do? Maybe I should just *go* to Kim's house. That way she'd have to see me. If I could just talk to her face to face—that's not gonna work. Her stupid mom would probably have me arrested before I got out of my car. Fuck. I know I can fix this. I can fix anything. I'm gonna play tonight and I'm not going to lose Susie over these *girls*. I can't. How am I going to keep this from the Colonel? I should just tell him straight out, take my chances with him, and hope that he can get me out of this. Yeah, right.

The Colonel, he'll love this.

He might be able to get me out of it, but that's a beating I'll never forget.

The past coming back now, strong. I try to push it away, but I can't. *Fuck you.* I said that to him, once. The Colonel looked at me like he was going to kill me. If it wasn't for the doorbell ringing, I think he might have. That pizza delivery boy probably saved my life. It wasn't the belt that time, it was his fists. Fat knuckles exploding into my belly. Exploding into my ribs. Exploding. I couldn't breathe. I couldn't feel anything. My legs went numb. I thought I was going to die.

The Colonel broke three ribs that night.

The Colonel.

Fuck you.

The bell rings . . .

Stew gives me the thumbs up, pushing his chair back, leaving class. I just stare right through him. Right through everyone. The past coming back strong, the past, coming back . . .

chapter 13

Principal Roberts: Where did you get this?

Floater: From his locker—

Roberts: I don't want to know how you got in . . .

Floater: I wasn't going to tell you.

Roberts: Good—God, this is some dark stuff. I didn't think Reynolds was *this* twisted.

Floater: You can never tell with these kids. Just when you think they couldn't be any more screwed up—

Roberts: Hey, Mark, how can you be so smug? *You* used to be one of *these* kids until I rescued you, remember? Let's not forget where you came from, Marky.

Floater: I'll never forget, sir. But that's ancient history. What's important is right now, and right now this kid is a threat. He's a threat to you, to me, and everyone else in this school. He needs to be stopped, sir.

Roberts: This kid really is twisted. What kind of sick mind is capable of thinking up this stuff?

Floater: It is shocking, isn't it. What do you want to do? Go straight to the cops?

Roberts: Are you kidding? Not on your life. We're going to handle this in-house, and very quietly. I'm going to call him down, have a little chat with him. See what he says when I confront him. Then I'm going to make sure he never sets foot in this school again. You know, now that I think of it, I'm going to call down this Tisha girl as well. He's got a lot of stuff about her in here. She must know him. She could be helpful.

Floater: A very wise decision, sir.

Roberts: Mark, you've outdone yourself this time. You may have saved us all with this. I owe you for this, Mark, I owe you big-time . . .

Floater: It was my pleasure, sir. Do you mind if I stick around awhile?

Roberts: Be my guest. I'll write you a note for your last class.

Floater: Thank you, sir. I appreciate it.

Roberts: I have to make a quick call. Have a seat; I'll be right back.

"I'm sorry, Ryan. I did everything I could. The alumni don't want to get involved. I even tried to call in some favors on the school board, but I struck out. Nobody wants to stick their necks out these days.

"They're going to let Ron do that, and let him sink or swim by himself. Every one of them said it was his call. They all sounded like a goddamn broken record.

"I don't know what to do. I really don't. It really looks like this thing is going to happen. I can't believe I'm saying this, but I don't think you're going to play tonight. I'm really worried now, Ryan. This thing with the girl, this is not good. It goes way beyond the game tonight. If this sexual assault charge stays on your transcripts, it's going to haunt you your whole life. Now, I believe you, I believe you when you say the girl is lying, but I don't know if me believing you is enough. I just don't know if it's going to be enough to get you out of this mess. And I'm talking in the long term. You're a good kid, Ryan. This is killing me, watching this thing happen to you. It really is.

"Are you sure you don't want me to call your dad? I really think he should know about all this. Maybe there's something—or maybe he knows somebody who can get this thing straightened out. What do you say, Ryan?"

I watch the coach's mouth moving. The words he's saying make me feel sick to my stomach. Sick. I'm trying to block the words out, but they keep coming. Blowing up in front of me. My whole life blowing up in front of my eyes. My whole life.

The coach is shaking his head as he talks. He looks defeated.

I've never seen the coach look like that. Even when we were getting slaughtered my freshman year, he never looked beat. But now, he looks like he lost. And if the coach thinks he's lost, then I've lost.

I feel like all the blood just left my head. I feel dizzy, like you do after you get your bell rung real good in a game. I want to sit down, but I'm afraid I'll never get up again. The coach is staring at me, waiting for an answer. I don't have any more answers. I don't have anything anymore.

He wants to tell the Colonel. He thinks the Colonel can help. The Colonel . . .

I open my mouth and say one word . . .

"No."

My time now . . .

He owes me. Did you hear that? Owes me big-time, were his exact words, I think. He might as well say, *Here's the keys to the kingdom.*

Finally, after all the years of eating shit, then being under Roberts's thumb.

My day has come.

Marky? He had to go *there*, didn't he? Bringing up the past. See, he did that to try to show me who's boss. He'll never be the boss of me.

I've been waiting for this day. I knew it would come. I knew it.

Now *I've* got the power. Me. Not some kid dunking my head in the toilet.

Not some stupid moron beating the shit out of me every day for my lunch money.

Not some mediocre man who calls himself the principal. No, *me. Floater.*

I've got the real power now. This is *my time.*

This is *my time now . . .*

8th period
Tisha

This is gonna suck without Tiny. I don't even feel like studying. I really wanted to cut up with her. She makes me laugh so hard . . .

I feel pretty good now.

I think Cheryl got the message, but what if she didn't? I can't worry about that. I can't worry about what *could* happen. I just have to think about now. And right now, I'm BORED. Maybe I'll just surf the Internet. Mrs. Fields won't know what I'm doin'. I'll just say I'm doin' research. She looks like she doesn't care at all what we do.

Mrs. Fields's got that Do Not Disturb look on her face. I know she hates to be here. Who would want to teach study hall? There's nothin' to teach. Whatever . . . tonight's gonna be cool, gonna' be real fun havin' Tiny there—

*"Would Tisha Reznick and Kurt Reynolds please report
to Principal Roberts's office. Tisha Reznick and Kurt
Reynolds, please report to Principal Roberts's office.
Thank you."*
Mom probably got locked out again. She's always forget-
ting her keys.
That's like the third time this month . . . Dag . . . Wonder
what *he* got called down for?

8th period
Kurt

Did they just call my name?
This is all I need today. I don't know why I didn't leave
last period. I could've just said I was sick. I was. I
could've just kept that pass and kept on walking . . .
I always make the wrong decisions.

What if I don't go? What are they gonna' do to me?
What? Kick me out of school? They'd be doing me a
favor.
They're not gonna do shit, 'cause I've got my gym bag,
and I will—
What do they want anyway? Probably just gonna hassle
me.

Might as well go. It's just a waste of time to be here.
Besides, Tisha's gonna be down there. I heard her name
being called, too. Doesn't matter. I won't say anything to
her. I suck. I will always suck . . .

"Do you still have your 'just in case,' son?"
The Colonel's words from this morning, playing over and
over in my head.
He gave it to me right after that Stiles kid got shot. The
Colonel thought I needed protection.
Everything was so crazy right after the shooting, I
could've snuck in a bazooka.
Took them a while to put up all the metal detectors.
It's been in the bottom of my locker for a year. Just sitting there, safely tucked away in the bottom of a bag I
never open.
I walk slowly to my locker. I guess the coach did the best
he could. But now it's up to me. My future is in my
hands. My head is throbbing. Sweat is running down my
cheeks. I feel ... different now. Not the way I usually do.
I feel ... almost strange, like this whole thing isn't really
happening. Like I'm watching a movie about someone else's
life being ruined. Some actor up on the screen. Not me.

*The actor is getting the crap beat out of him, too. This
actor who looks so much like me. He's trying not to flinch,
always trying not to flinch as the blows rain down on him.
Blow after blow ... The actor is alone in his room, sitting in
a chair. He wants to cry, but he has no tears. The word escapes
the actor's lips. He says the word for the first time. "Abuse."*

I try to shake the movie out of my head. I slam my
locker shut and start walking, not really knowing where
I'm going to end up.

Not really knowing at all.

I crank up PANIC ATTAAK.
Nothing is bad when I've got the ATTAAK on . . .
I feel good.
I feel ready . . .
Me and Misty Manic on our way to the office.
Me and Misty Manic, ready for anything.
Me and
Misty Manic—screaming my favorite song.

Crash and burn
Something is wrong
Kill to learn
What's going on . . . ?
I'm a weapon, I'm a weapon, I'm a weapon, I'm a
weapon
of . . .
MASS
DESTRUCTION!
MASS
DESTRUCTION!!

YEAH!!   YEAH!!

YEAH!!   YEAH!!

AHHHHHHHHHHHHHHHH!!!!!!

Gloria Tinsley, Principal Roberts's Assistant: Are you Reznick?

Tisha: Yeah, I'm Tisha Reznick.

Mrs. Tinsley: Okay. Just have a seat. He'll be with you in a minute.

Tisha: Did my mom get locked out again? She called, right?

Mrs. Tinsley: No, as far as I know, your mom didn't call.

Tisha: Do you know why he wants to see me, then?

Mrs. Tinsley: They don't tell me much around here. All I know is that he'll be with you soon.

Tisha: Okay.

Mrs. Tinsley: Excuse me, you can't go in there. He's in a meeting. Hey, are you deaf?

Tisha: I guess he didn't hear you.

Mrs. Tinsley: Oh, he heard me. They always *hear* me. Problem is, nobody ever *listens* to me around here. Mr.

Roberts is not going to be happy about this. I don't know who he thinks I am. I'm not security or anything. I'll tell you, Reznick, they don't pay me near enough to deal with all the stuff that goes on in this place. Not near enough—well, there he is, calling me already. I told you he wasn't going to be happy about it.

Hello, Mr. Roberts, how can I *help* you . . . ?

Number 10

I'm here, my second home, the football locker room.
Staring at the big Number 10 pasted on my locker.
Number 10. That used to be me.
Number 10 should be the starting quarterback tonight.
Right now, Number 10 should be laughing with his girl-
friend. Holding hands, kissing . . .
This is not supposed to happen to me.
This is not supposed to happen to Number 10.
I've got my head between my legs, sitting on this bench,
all the blood rushing to my brain, like waves crashing
against rocks. I'm trying to smash away anything and
everything I can think of. I don't want to think. I don't
want to know anything.

*"Would Ryan Duncan please report to Principal
Roberts's office immediately. Ryan Duncan report to
Principal Roberts's office immediately."*

I hear the muffled voice of Mr. Roberts's secretary. I hear
my name. Maybe he changed his mind. Maybe I can play

tonight. I lift my head up. The blood flowing back to the rest of my body. I stand up slowly, trying to snap out of it. Maybe things will work out.

Maybe . . .

"Would Ryan Duncan please report to Principal Roberts's office immediately. Ryan Duncan report to Principal Roberts's office immediately."

chapter 14

My gym bag is on my lap. I am holding on to it with both hands. I wonder if it looks strange, how I'm holding it so tight. Tisha is sitting right next to me.

Now I'm starting to freak. What if they know? All that stuff I wrote. And there's stuff about Tisha, too. Not anything bad, but. What if she gets into trouble because of me? *Well, Kurt, you've done it again. Get the girl you really like in trouble with the principal. That would have to be the loser move of the century.* I try to force the thought out of my head. I try to force it out. Looking around I notice the bull pen is pretty empty. Just me and Tisha and a couple other kids way down at the other end. This big-ass area where students are herded like cattle, put in seats, and told to wait to see one of the VP's or the man himself, Principal Roberts. All the kids call it the bull pen, like in baseball. But if you get sent down here, it's not to pitch. It usually means detention, or worse . . . Didn't used to be all open like this, but they redid it after the murder last year. They said it was more secure like this.

Roberts's secretary looks nervous. She's not looking at anyone. Her head's buried in some papers. All the loud yelling coming from the office is not making me feel any better about being here.

NO WAY! Tisha's smile takes me by surprise; she's staring right at me. She looks like she's going to say something to me. Those beautiful lips, and the way her cheeks rise up so high on her face . . . I loosen my grip on my gym bag. I should just put it on the floor, like a normal person . . . but I can't. I have to have my gym bag close. I might have to do something. I am so close. So close to doing something, so close to doing what I think about doing every day . . . What I've thought about doing every day since I stopped being me and became Dirt. I hate Dirt. I wish Dirt was dead. I want to be me again, like I used to be. Maybe the time has come. Time to take a stand. Get rid of the ones who keep me down. Maybe this is how I can be me again. Start at the top. Why not? I could do it, I could . . .

Even with Tisha next to me, I could do it . . . Just calmly walk into his office, unzip my gym bag, and—

"So what are *you* down here for?" I wasn't expecting to hear her voice. My heart starts beating fast; my face gets flushed. For a minute, I think I was speaking out loud. All my thoughts out in the open for her to hear.

It takes me a few seconds to realize she is speaking to *me*. I instinctively look over my shoulder, expecting someone else to be there, the person she's actually speaking to. BUT no one is there. Just me. She is *speaking* to *me*. All of a sudden I feel embarrassed. I lower my gym bag to the floor and shift in my seat. Say something back; just say anything . . . I turn towards Tisha and smile. My mouth opens, welcoming the words that are about to come out.

The yelling in the office is getting louder . . .

"I don't know. They just called me dow—" The sound of the office door being slammed open stops everything in the bull pen.

Roberts's secretary lets out a scream. Tisha looks horrified. I am just pissed I didn't get a chance to finish my sentence . . . I *never* catch a break.

Tisha

"So what are *you* down here for?" As soon as I say it, I wish I'd said it differently. I hope I didn't sound like I thought he was in trouble or something. I just wanted to say something. Shoot, *I'm* probably in trouble, and I don't even know what I did. I should really thank Kurt for helping me pick up my books that time. He probably doesn't remember anyway. What's he lookin' at? He's so shy . . . Dag, what's goin on in the principal's office? Kurt's got a nice smile; he should smile more. I should tell him that. That would be a good thing to say . . .

"I don't know. They just called me dow—" I feel myself jump back in my chair. I want to run out of here but I can't move. My heart is beating a million miles an hour. That door was so loud. Slamming against the wall, the sound was sickening. Mrs. Tinsley's scream gives me a chill down my back. I wish I could scream. I can't do anything but sit here, frozen like a big block of ice. I feel like I'm going to be sick.
Sometimes I throw up when I get scared . . .
I really hope I don't throw up.

I wish Tiny was here . . .

Floater

I feel the warmth before I feel the wetness. Now the dark spot forms, but I'm the only one who seems to notice. The fact that I've just pissed myself is the last thing on anyone's mind in this office. I can't catch my breath, and I feel like I'm going to puke. My hand is shaking and sweat is pouring down my face. To look at me, you'd think I was just sprayed with a garden hose.

This is the first time in my life that I'm actually *not* hungry. I haven't eaten since seven this morning, but the thought of food is making me gag. Why the hell didn't I leave earlier? I didn't have to stay, but I *had* to see what happened.

Had to see the fruits of my labor. Fuck me. So full of myself standing there leaning against Roberts's desk, touching it like it was my prize. Both of us congratulating each other on our impending victory. Damn, I should've left when I had the chance. So stupid of me. And now—

"You've got piss running down your leg, son. What kind of weak faggot are you?" I guess someone did notice. The crazed man's voice pushes me back, like an unseen force, pushing me back into Roberts's desk.

I call him the crazed man, but we know who he is, don't we?

Colonel James P. Duncan, decorated war hero, respected member of the community. Complete psycho.

"You make me sick, boy." Colonel Duncan has the blade of the knife pushed against Roberts's Adam's apple. From the look of the few drops of blood collecting under Roberts's chin, I'd say the thing is sharp. Colonel Duncan orders us to stand in front of the office door, our backs to him. This is not good . . . I am trying to pretend this isn't really happening; it can't be. It's too fucked up. This crazed bastard has totally fucked everything up.

Everything I've worked for, all those twisted moments,

leading up to what should have been my coming-out party. Now he's about to piss it all away. Actually, he's making me piss it all away. If I could do something, I would, but I can't. I am powerless. I can't call anyone, get some thug to do my dirty work for me. No, all I can do is just stand here and piss on myself. Standing at attention. Watching Colonel Duncan get ready to slice up my ticket to paradise.

The sound of the office door slamming against the wall makes my ears ring. I almost fall on my face as I get pushed out into the bull pen.

If I could still pee, there would be a flood on the floor by now.

I glance over at Roberts; he looks like a man who has given up.

He looks like he knows the end is coming soon.

Fuck that. I'm not giving up. I've been through too much to have it end like this.

Too much . . .

Ryan

I'm feeling better. Better with every step I take, on my way to the office. Things are going to be alright. Roberts backed down. I knew he would. I knew I would win; Duncans always win—

I hear the voice before I see the face. I know instantly who it is. Everything I had hoped for just five seconds ago is gone. It's all gone.

I stop short of the bull pen. Staying out of sight.

Kids are starting to come out of classrooms, wondering what all the noise is about. I take a quick peek into the bull pen. The scene that greets me is a complete freak show but I shouldn't be surprised. He finally snapped. The crazy bastard finally snapped. I see the knife just for a few seconds. Shit, that's his combat knife. An original F.S. fighting knife from World War II. Told me he got it at an auction. He called it a killing blade . . .

I am hit with the sudden realization of what I have to do. Everything is clear. *This has to stop.* The words on the tip of my tongue. *This has to stop.* Now they come out, in a whisper. *This has to stop.*

I take two steps forward, his words becoming clear now. I don't hear him.

I don't care what he's saying. It doesn't matter anyway. It's too late for words.

Too late . . .

Floater

"GET THE GODDAMN PAPERS OR I'M GOING TO SLIT HIS THROAT."

Mrs. Tinsley is pretending to rummage through her desk, looking for the imaginary papers that will pardon the Duncan kid.

That psycho told Roberts he was going to give him one chance to fix everything. When a maniac comes into your office and says he's going to give you a chance, you say

Okay. You don't tell him there's nothing you can do. You're supposed to lie *before* the knife is at your throat. Doesn't he ever go to the movies? Now this bogus paper hunt. How long does he think Colonel Crazy is going to go for this? Not very long. Roberts is such a moron.

"WHERE ARE THOSE GODDAMN PAPERS?"

I must look like shit. Piss all over myself, and right in front of Tisha.

I wonder if she read my note yet? I could make a break for it, but I'd never make three feet. That crazy fuck would slice us both up before I even got my fat ass to the hallway. OUCH, fucker's twisting my arm.

He spins me and Roberts around, so we're facing the entrance to the bull pen. He's still behind us, but now he's standing next to Mrs. Tinsley's desk.

She's shuffling papers frantically. There's no way she can keep this up much longer.

Where the hell is security, they should be here by now . . .

Tisha

"WHERE ARE THOSE GODDAMN PAPERS?"

This seems like a real bad movie playing right in front of me. But I know this is real; this is not a movie. This is really happening. All I can think of is Jake. Dead on the bathroom floor. Pools of blood collecting around his mouth. Every detail of that morning coming back. Coming back so clear it's like it's happening all over again. I'm not gonna end up like him, no way. I can't let this go on. I must be crazy, too, but I can't let this guy do this. I can do something. I know I can. If I don't do something, this guy is going to kill us all. We're *all* gonna end up like Jake.

He's probably got something more than just that knife. He's got that look in his eyes, like he doesn't care. *Now* he's got Principal Roberts and that Mark kid—facing the *other* way. The crazy man's back is to me.

Maybe I can sneak up on him. Maybe . . .

"Kurt, I'm going to do something. I have to stop this." I stand up, almost instinctively.

"Tisha, don't." Kurt looks scared. He looks like he can't believe I'm standing. I can't either. Kurt shakes his head, staring at me like I'm out of my mind. Maybe I am but I have to go through with this.

"Tisha, are you crazy? Don't, he'll kill you. Just wait, wait . . . I have a plan."

"Really?" I whisper back. I think he'd tell me anything at this point.

Kurt is begging me to sit down. If he could scream it, I'm sure he would. The guy is getting angrier. He's getting even louder, pushing that Mark kid around. I can't stop thinking about how his uniform has no wrinkles. Its perfect, everything in place. Every medal shining on his lapel. He looks so professional, he looks so together . . . Why is he acting so crazy? . . . My bravery tries to slip away. I won't let it, but reality is sinking in.

How do you stop a crazy man?
I finally sit down and whisper to Kurt, "What are you gonna do?"
He doesn't say anything.
I hope it's a good plan.
A real good plan . . .

chapter 15

"WHERE ARE THOSE GODDAMN PAPERS?"

His voice is gravelly, like a smoker who has screamed his whole life.

His eyes are what I see first, darting wildly in all directions. Then I see the knife. It looks like one of those knives from an old war movie.

Long skinny blade . . . Looks sharp as hell.

The blade is making little flashes of light from the high-beam fluorescents hitting it from above.

Damn, that dude looks mean. Roberts looks like he's afraid he's gonna die. He's got that look like he's already dead.

The kid's got a big wet spot on his pants. Serves him right. I hate that kid; he's that snitch, always thinks he's better than everyone else, too. The guy looks like he's a military officer or something. He's got ribbons and stuff on his jacket, and he's got one of those cool beret hats I saw on that *Killer Combat* show. The soldier guy's got the knife under Roberts's chin and he keeps pushin' the kid and pullin' his arm back. He turns them around. Damn, he must be strong. He barely notices me and Tisha, sitting behind him. He just keeps screaming at the secretary about some papers. This dude is whacked.

He looks crazy, but kinda cool at the same time.

"Kurt, I'm going to do something. I have to stop this."

"Tisha, don't." Tisha is halfway out of her chair before I can get the words out of my mouth.

"Tisha, are you crazy? Don't, he'll kill you. Just wait, wait . . . I have a plan."

"Really?" She sounds like she doesn't believe me.

"Yeah, but you have to sit down. Come on, sit back down." Now I'm pleading with her. Slowly she sits back down. Fortunately, the soldier guy is too busy yelling to notice what's going on.

I have a plan. Yeah, right. I had to say something. She was gonna get herself killed. What was she gonna do anyway? Man, that girl is brave.

"What are you gonna do?" Tisha whispers. I don't answer.

My gym bag is under my chair. I push it very slowly with both feet, bringing it forward. I can tell Tisha is watching what I'm doing.

Why should I risk my life for Roberts and his little snitch? What did they ever do for me? I *know* they wouldn't save my ass if the situation was reversed.

But Tisha, she was going to actually try to stop that crazy dude. She is so amazing.

What the *hell* am I gonna do?

R y a n

"I WANT THOSE GODDAMN PAPERS AND I WANT THEM RIGHT NOW.

"WHERE THE HELL IS MY SON! YOU BETTER GET ME MY SON! DO NOT UNDERESTIMATE MY RESOLVE."

He's screaming like a maniac. He's really lost it now. He sounds crazier than I've ever heard him. He's so full of shit. He doesn't give a crap about me. This is just fun for him. Sick fun.

Well, I'm about to rain on his twisted parade . . . two more steps and I'm in. Two more steps . . .

"I'm right here, sir. Drop the knife and let them go. Do not underestimate *my* resolve."

Floater

Shoot the crazy bastard. I said that in my head. I wanted to say it out loud, but the way things are going for me, the gun's probably not even loaded.

Ryan looks too calm, too in control. I don't like that. I think he's going to do it. I think he's really gonna off his old man. He looks like he could shoot us all.

I really hope that thing isn't loaded. Looks like a Glock— how did he get that thing into school anyway? Past the metal detectors? They never check the jocks.

Fuck, does it even matter now?

I should've left when I had the chance . . . Now everything is fucked. I can't get my money from the geek squad, my great plan evaporating right before my eyes. And . . .

my lovely Tisha . . .

oh, Tisha . . .

"Where did you get that, son?"

"You gave it to me, remember? My 'just in case'?"

"I don't know what you're talking about, but I'm giving you about five seconds to give me that gun or you're going to be really sorry."

"Sorry? Sorry for what? Sorry that you're my father? Sorry that you regularly beat the shit out of me for no reason? Sorry because you don't even care about *me,* really? All you care about is Ryan Duncan, the all-American football player. The only reason you're here is because of *you,* not me. You just want the glory; you just want to be able to say that I'm your kid, be able to tell all your buddies how you made me, how it was all because of you . . . Well, you can tell *this* to your buddies. I fucked up. That's right, Mr. Roberts. Kim told the truth. I did what they said I did. I'm really a fuckup, Dad. I can't control myself. I have a problem—I have problems. How do you like that, huh? Your perfect son is really a fuckup. What do you think of that?"

"You don't know what you're saying. They've got you all turned around. It's this damn school, all these faggots runnin' around . . ."

"It's not the school; it's me. It's me. You know why I'm the way I am? Because I learned everything I know from

you. You're *so* warped. Look at you; you're a disgrace.
A disgrace to yourself, to your family, to your country.
What would Mom think if she was here? You're a dis-
grace to her memory—"

"You'd better watch that mouth, son. Now drop your
weapon or I will put you in a world of hurt. Drop your
weapon. That is a direct order."

"I already *am* in a world of hurt. What the hell can you
do to me now? No matter what I did . . . captain of the
football team, an all-American . . . you never said shit—
not one thing that ever made me think you loved me,
even a little bit—nothin'. Nothin' but your belt. Well,
fuck it. I'm sick of all this shit, and it's all gonna stop
right now. So I'm going to tell you one last time, put
down the knife and let them go.

"*That* is a direct order. Do not underestimate *my*
resolve."

Dark and quiet

I don't even remember getting up. It was all in super-
super slow motion. Tisha turning to me, nodding her
head, like she knew what I was going to do before I did.
Me, looking at this totally bizarre scene playing itself out.
Knowing that this was not going to have a happy ending.
Realizing that soldier boy is standing with his back to me.
Completely oblivious to the fact that I am sitting right
behind him.

The captain of the football team, screaming and pointing that gun into his father's face. I don't think he'd notice if the roof fell in.

I don't remember getting up. But before I know it, I am UP. On my feet *swinging* my gym bag at the back of the crazy man's head. *Swinging* like I had a Louisville slugger and it was the bottom of the ninth. *Swinging* with all of my hate, and anger, and fear, *swinging* at the heads of everyone who ever cut me—put me—DOWN—turned me into Dirt, turned me into Dirt . . . *Swinging* . . . I watch the crazy man stagger to his left, falling—fast over the desk, the knife flying out of his hands, landing safely away. He just misses the secretary as he crashes to the floor. Roberts races out of the bull pen, the snitch who peed himself right behind. I see Tisha out of the corner of my eye, standing up, moving towards me . . .

I hear screams and yelling and running getting closer—sounding like an army approaching.

Sprinting into the bull pen, they tackle the quarterback first. Then they jump on top of that crazy man. I don't move, I can't.

I feel the weight of someone big on my back. Before I know it, I am at the bottom of a big pile. Bodies on top of me grabbing and punching . . .

I can't breathe. I can't breathe . . .

Then
everything stops.
No motion, no sound.
Nothing.
Everything is dark.

Everything is
dark
and
quiet.

chapter 16

Floater's walk . . .

This is Mandy Montgomery, reporting live from Rockville High School, where on the one-year anniversary of the murder of Jake Stiles, yet another tragedy was just barely averted. Details are still sketchy but what we do know is that a crazed parent took the principal and a student hostage . . .

In a bizarre twist, the crazed parent was apparently confronted by his son, who had a gun . . . I will have more on this developing story throughout the afternoon . . .

I'm walking . . . Walking past everything and everyone . . . Cameras and reporters, cops, firemen . . .
Mandy Montgomery looks like a little kid on Christmas day. She must live for this stuff. I smell like piss and sweat, and I've never been so hungry in my life.
But I don't stop, not for Mandy, not for the cops, not even for Tisha.
I'm just going to keep walking, keep walking all the way home . . .

Then I'm going to eat everything in the house . . .

Tisha in the car . . .

Mom is so scared, I can see her hands shaking on the steering wheel . . . She hasn't stopped hugging me since I got in the car . . . That Mark kid looks like he just came back from a war or something . . . The police said we could go home, for now. I didn't see what happened to Kurt. They were on top of him so fast, then it was just a blur . . . Everything happening all at once . . . I hope he doesn't get in trouble.

They took Principal Roberts away in an ambulance . . . they said just for observation..

Mom is crying now . . . She's got Dad on the cell phone . . . I'm sooooo tired . . .

I'm just glad I'm alive . . .

Tiny is going to trip when she hears about this . . . She is going to *trip* . . .

The wicked witch is dead.

"I had to do it. I didn't have a choice."

"I didn't have a choice . . ." I'm trying to convince the paramedic who's stitching my eye that I had to pull a gun on my own father. He is nodding his head, like you might do to a crazy person. My back is itching, but I can't scratch it because of the handcuffs . . . The paramedic is talking to me now, speaking slowly like I was a child. Like I really *was* crazy . . .

But, I know I'm not crazy. I've never felt saner in my life. Fuckin' security smashed up my eye really good.

I didn't even see them coming.

All I saw was that kid whackin' the Colonel in the back of the head with his gym bag . . . What was in that thing? Man, that took balls . . . That kid, I don't even know his name . . . The dude must have ice water in his veins . . .

They say I might get charged, but I don't care . . . I'm free . . . The wicked witch is dead.
The twisted Colonel is going to jail . . . That's good enough for me . . . I hope he rots . . .

A Hero is born

Mandy: This is Mandy Montgomery reporting live from Rockville High School, where new details are emerging from this afternoon's near tragedy . . .

Everyone is looking at me, but it's different now . . . They think I saved them . . . They're saying things, pointing and staring at me . . . But in a different way . . . Where's Tisha? I really want to talk to her . . . If it wasn't for her—I hope this doesn't take too long—Wow, Mandy is even hotter up close . . .

Mandy: The hero student's name is Kurt Reynolds, and we are lucky enough to have him right here. Kurt, can you tell us in your own words what happened? I understand you were the one who actually knocked the knife out of Colonel Duncan's hands. How did you do it? How does it feel to be a hero? Your parents must be so proud. Is there anything you want to say to them? Do you have anything to say to the youth of America?

The bright lights are blinding. It hurts to open my eyes all the way . . . Told me to go talk to Mandy. They said I was going to be on TV . . I just want to go home . . . Can you believe that? All I want to do is go home, lay my head down, and sleep . . . Just sleep . . .

Mandy: Kurt, we are *live,* you know. Do you have anything to say to them? The youth of America?

Kurt: What do I have to say to the youth of America?

Good luck . . .

c o d a

It's midnight and I can't sleep. This could very well be my last night on earth. My last night as Floater. The late word is that Roberts is going to get fired. The McConnell girl's charge, the murder last year . . . and with what happened today with that psycho . . . Too many hits to take . . . no one could survive that. Not even crafty Ronny Roberts. There's going to be a housecleaning, top to bottom. Maybe the whole administration.

That notebook thing blew up in my face, too. I got a call from one of my "sources." Can you believe somebody snitched on *me*? What is this world coming to. Some kid claims he saw me take the notebook from Kurt's locker. He said he saw me writing in it. Kid went and told Vice-Principal Shavers. You know Shavers will try to use this to save his own butt. He's on a sinking ship, every man for himself. Oh, well, I guess "hero boy" Kurt will be around a little longer.

Hey, I tried. Don't blame me when that time bomb goes off. Doesn't matter, I won't be around for the fallout.

Tomorrow morning a new day will dawn. An entirely different reality, a different universe where I no longer exist. Well, to be perfectly honest, a place where I couldn't exist. Even if Roberts stayed, how could I? How could I go back to just being Mark Daniels, junior at Rockville High? Just another nameless fat-faced loser with the added tag of the kid who pissed himself when the going got a little tough. No, not me, not after everything I've been through . . . Tomorrow morning is something I've dreaded for a long time, but it's not something I haven't planned for. One thing you should remember is that I'm always a step ahead. Oh yeah, I've made my calls, given my mom the old sob story. "I don't feel safe anymore at Rockville. I am emotionally scarred by the day's events." She bought it.

If things go the way I hope they do, in a week I will be enrolled at Norwood. How does the saying go? The enemy of my enemy is my friend? Our arch rivals and future state champs . . .

Hey, free enterprise, and I go to the highest bidder. From what I understand, they are in need of someone with some very specific skills. Someone who can get them what they need, someone who can keep the peace . . . I heard they need a new pair of ears, a new set of eyes, their man on the inside . . . Someone like . . . Floater. There will be sacrifices to make, Tisha for one, but . . . I suppose: "Just knowing she is in the world will have to be enough . . ." At least for now.

Now

I have to keep my eye on the prize . . . With Roberts getting all the heat, I get off scot-free. I've got no shit on my shoes, just a little piss in my pants . . . I am still the man with the golden tongue, Johnny-on-the-spot.

The ultimate weapon—the new twenty-first-century spy.

Don't cry for me. I'll be alright.

You know why?

Because, I'm a genius

and I'm beyond you . . .

remember . . .

It's gonna be OK

I'm gonna make everything right, with Susie . . . with Kim . . . I'm gonna get help . . . I need help; I know that now . . . It's been too much, all these years . . . fighting this war . . . It's just been too much . . . But now it's over. The war is finally over. I'll get Susie back; I'll play again . . .

I know I will.

It's gonna be OK. I really think it's gonna be OK . . .

"LIGHTS OUT."

Beginning

I'm upstairs in my secret lair. Been watching Kurt all night, on all the stations. He mentioned my name every time. He said I was the one who gave him the courage to stop Colonel Duncan. That was real cool, but I don't know if it's true. Tiny called, to make sure I was alright. I didn't feel like going out tonight. Tiny said she was too upset to eat. Too worried about me.

I talked to Kurt a little while ago. It was real nice to talk to him. Real nice . . .

I'm so tired. I can't even think straight.

Mom and Dad said I was brave. They said they love me so much.

They said a lot through their tears . . .

I haven't even cried yet. Is that weird?

Somethin's changed, though . . .

I feel different now.
Somethin' changed *me* in the bull pen today.
I don't feel as afraid; I don't feel as lost. I don't feel like
I'll melt away in the sun.

I'm beginning to know who I am now.

I'm beginning to know

who I am . . .

Hope

I am home. Under the covers. Lights are out.
I was interviewed by six different news stations tonight.
Mandy Montgomery gave me an autographed picture of
herself. It's up on my wall, next to my poster of Misty
Manic riding a Harley.

My parents are treating me different now, like I'm a
star, like I did something really important. That was a
quick change. Maybe I'll give them the benefit of the
doubt. At least for now.

It was so great to talk to Tisha tonight. Maybe I *will* get
the girl, like in the movies. Maybe I will . . .

I'm so tired, I could sleep for days. I'm supposed to be
on The Morning Show tomorrow with Tisha. That should
be real cool, if I get up in time.

My gym bag is under my bed now; no one even looked
inside.

Man, they would have been surprised . . .

Mr. Tanner called me. He said that I was a hero. I told him I didn't know what that meant. I told him I just did what I did. What I had to do.
He said that he was proud of me and that I was a very special person.
Special, no one's ever called me that before . . . I like that . . . I like being special . . .

I feel good, like I used to when I was younger. I feel like it's the past, only it's the present. Does that make any sense? I want to keep this feeling. I want to always feel like this, like I'm OK and things are going to be OK and I'm not going to have to eat shit every day and my parents will understand me more, and . . . not ignore me and . . . everything will be like it was . . .
Like it is now.
I hope this feeling lasts forever . . .

I hope . . .